BAD COP

PETER SARDA

The characters and events in this book are fictitious. Any similarity to real persons, living or dead, is coincidental and not intended.

Cover design by Phil Poole.

ISBN 978-3-9824312-3-9

99 Highway 99 Press

Contents

Prologue

Noah opened the battered Deutsche Grammophon case, pulled out the first CD, slipped it into the ghetto blaster, and skipped to the fifth track, Vivaldi's *Concerto No. 8 for Two Violins in A Minor*. "Ready?" he said, his bow hovering above the violin grasped by his shoulder and jaw. The smell of resin on horsehair made his scalp tingle in anticipation.

After a few cracks and pops of the digitally remastered recording, he felt a burst of energy. He lifted his instrument dramatically to signal to his partner. Together they began playing the joyful music, sending sweet signals to each other like lovers dancing through a meadow.

Her summer dress whirled above the bright yellow rapeseed carpeting the fecund earth of the lush valley. He threw her into the bright blue sky—and was blinded momentarily by the midday sun—only to catch her in his arms effortlessly.

He didn't need eyes to see. They read each other like braille. Fathers and daughters. In some ways, they were closer than husbands and wives.

The two of them danced through the bright field, one taking the lead, then the other. The rest of the players danced along with them, whirling and twirling their instruments into the air. Tubas turned end over end in slow motion, cellos whirled above their heads, only to return to their owners in time for their cues.

Noah hardly noticed, so intent was he on the subtle interplay with his daughter, who was glowing with rapture. Only the bunching of her dark eyebrows revealed her deep concentration. But even that finally gave way to the levity, rising with the high notes and delicate passages as their eyes met in an exquisite moment of unspoken unity. They were at one with themselves and each other.

The CD crackled to a peaceful analog end, proving once again that it was recorded before her time. She loved that almost as much as he loved her.

The intensity of the empty silence that followed burned Noah's eyes, but only for a moment, as refreshing tears of joy streamed down his face, cooling his burning skin. He knew she was with him in her heart.

His tears turned to uncontrollable sobbing that shook his shoulders violently. He sank to the ground, holding onto the bedsheet for dear life.

There was a rush of cold air at his back. The polished floor squeaked. Someone grabbed his shoulders gently but firmly, almost lifting him to his feet. "You have to go, sir. Now."

Loud beeping noises were coming from the flashing machines above his daughter's head. Oh God.

He barely recognized her with all the tubes sticking out of her. His precious little baby was just staring emptily at the ceiling, a living corpse, no thought in her dark brown eyes, no feeling in her cold hands. A hideous white tube taped to her mouth pumped oxygen into her chest with a sickening sucking and banging that smashed his soul. The too-white machines flashed lights and numbers, tracking the forced rhythm of her rising and falling chest. Large white rails prevented her comatose body from falling out of the bed. It was hideous.

"Oh God!" he screamed. "What have they done to my baby?"

. . .

"I don't know how to tell you this," Noah said, placing the white quartz pebble on top of the gravestone. He had left enough room for two more etched forenames. He choked back tears. Never in a million years did he think his own name would be the third in line. Everything was wrong. The world was upside down.

He concentrated on the white pebble. It told him that his wife was still with him, here, on earth, to give him strength in this time of unbearable sorrow. "I did everything I could," he said, wiping his eyes.

Then he brightened. "You remember how I brought her licorice? You know, the red ones she liked so much? The doctors said smell was the strongest sense of all. It was the best way of getting to her." He knew his wife had heard it dozens of times, but he said it anyway. He was reminding himself as much as her.

In those early days, his daughter's nostrils quivered at the sticky strands of red licorice tantalizing them. He didn't so much see the quivering as feel it. She was there. He just knew it!

The memories came flooding in. The way little Sarah, age seven, grabbed the chewy stuff with her gappy teeth, pulled it until it broke, and then gnawed on it with a big grin on her freckly face.

"She always knew what she wanted," Noah said. The fold-up beach chair squeaked as he adjusted his weight.

"After smell therapy we tried stories, remember?" he said. "You told me to start with *Grimm's Fairy Tales*. You said we could sneak in some smell therapy because Opa Goldberg's big book was so musty." He laughed. "That was *so* you. You and Sarah. My two little women. You both thought the same. Always trying to trick the system and raise the stakes. Always getting ahead of the game."

Like the music lessons. That was Sarah's idea, of course. When she turned seven, she announced that she was learning to play the violin. Somehow, she'd found a private teacher in the neighborhood. Already she was "practicing" by imitating what she heard on the stereo with the baby violin she'd picked out for her birthday. She even had a book and CD called *Listen and Play*. Her teacher called it the Suzuki Method. Her first big hit was "Twinkle, Twinkle Little Star." She listened and played and listened and played until the little star twinkled just right.

But things really took off with Vivaldi. One bright Saturday morning, Noah was reading the newspaper in his overstuffed chair, his feet on the matching footrest, listening to *Concerto No. 8*. It reminded him of his grandparents. He sighed happily as the two violinists jumped in together, playing the joyous music like they were extensions of each other. After a moment, he heard a kind of echo. He looked up from the paper at the old turntable.

The black shiny vinyl was making the needle wobble as it slowly turned around and around. Nearby, two small tap-dancing shoes were keeping time on the carpet. His daughter, still wearing her pink ballerina costume from *Cinderella* rehearsal at school, was pulling her tiny bow across the strings of her miniature violin. Her brows furrowed in concentration as her little fingers flew across the strings in time to the music. Sometimes, she hit the right notes half a beat after the two violinists.

Noah almost fell out of his chair, despite the arms. His little girl was playing Vivaldi! Passage by passage, she followed the record's lead, with near misses gradually becoming hits. As the two violinists increased their pace and intensity, little Sarah did the same, with alarming accuracy. Noah blinked rapidly. His mouth was too dry to call out to his wife. It was a miracle!

In retrospect, they realized it was inevitable. DNA was destiny.

Music ran in the Goldberg family—even if it skipped a generation or two. Noah certainly didn't have the ear or the skill, despite eight years of tedious lessons and practice while all the other kids played soccer outside. On his sixteenth birthday, he was allowed to quit. Then came little Sarah with her *Cinderella* costume and her baby violin. She more than made up for his failure.

Noah looked at the framed photo browning gracefully behind protective glass over the mantle. His grandmother was resting her head on his grandfather's lap with those big eyes of hers. His grandfather appeared to be reading a book out loud. The two of them were dressed formally but lounging on their big, quilted bed. Opa Goldberg was a violinist, Oma Goldberg a cellist. Both were members of the Hamburg Philharmonic, performing regularly in the Laeiszhalle until 1933.

Sarah was fascinated by the sculptures that decorated the Baroque Revival music hall. She called it the "curly cue place." But what made her eyebrows really furrow was the sights and sounds inside. She always "directed," standing at the front railing of the balcony. There was no holding her back. The other members of the audience didn't mind. Many seemed relieved by the distraction. Some even called her "the little director." Sarah didn't disagree with the title.

Noah's eyes traced the beautiful curves of the elegant Garamond script chiseled into the tombstone. Sarah had especially loved what she called the hands and feet on the letters.

"Like you always said, we're investing in our future," Noah said. His wife was right about everything, especially Sarah.

Then Noah remembered the hideous tubes and beeping in the hospital. His throat caught painfully. He leaned forward, sinking to the thick grass and clutching it with both hands. "What have they done to our baby," he sobbed, rocking on hands and knees damp with morning dew.

ONE
Lone Wolf

Kriminalhauptkommissar Wolf spotted the dealer in his usual spot, sandwiched between two underage whores on a horseshoe couch in the far corner of the narrow, backlit bar, the wall mirror to their back. Hidden speakers were whispering a 1970s disco hit. It sounded like the soundtrack to "Saturday Night Fever."

Wolf smirked. St. Pauli never disappointed. He brushed past girls perched on shiny stools in glow-in-the-dark pastel bikinis and matching high heels that showed off voluptuous salon tans to their elderly "dates."

"Hey, scumbag," he said, walking up to the couch. It looked incandescent under the black light, but he knew it was pink velvet. "Where's my cut?"

The alarm in the dealer's eyes was immediately covered by reptilian lids. He shooed away his female companions with a large pinky ring and clunky bracelet. "What cut?"

Wolf pulled out his SIG Sauer P6, cocked it, and slammed the barrel onto the dealer's thigh. "This cut," he said and pulled the trigger. The sound of the blast was muffled by pulverized femur—and followed by screams.

The loudest came from the dealer, who was writhing on the red carpet, clutching his smoking thigh with both hands.

"Where's my cut?" Wolf repeated, pressing the bloody mess of flesh, bone, and black leather with a steel shank.

The guttural agony under his boot got even louder.

Wolf regretted his carelessness. It would take more than saddle soap to clean his carefully oiled Red Wings. Son of a bitch. He increased the pressure on the wound.

The scream went up an octave under the flashing disco lights.

The rest of the bar averted its gaze. The whores and johns knew the drill. Nobody in St. Pauli ever saw anything that might jeopardize their own health. From the hidden speakers, the Bee Gees underlined the point with their falsetto "Stayin' Alive."

Wolf reached down and frisked the leather jacket at his feet with latex-gloved fingers. He came up with three small baggies. Each contained identical amounts of yellow powder. He figured a gram apiece. He opened one baggie carefully and dipped a finger inside. His tongue tingled disapproval. The meth was probably cut with baby laxative. He sighed. It would have to do until his next visit to the property room.

Wolf holstered his gun and sauntered over to the bar, barely registering the whores and johns making a scared, silent exit out the front door. He lifted a slightly warped plank that felt sticky, stepped onto the spongy black rubber mat, and turned sideways to slip through a narrow doorway hidden behind a black curtain.

In the stuffy back room, he spotted a fifth of Jack Daniels and a carton of unfiltered Camels. They were his now. He retraced his steps and hit the front door. Kool & the Gang were blasting "Open Sesame" as the evening air cooled his face.

Wolf chuckled and headed for the alley, which was keeping the beat by spraying beams of white neon across the tailfins of the glistening metallic-brown Mercedes. His old man, who drove the 220 SE off the factory floor in 1968, wouldn't have approved of the blinking titties and spread legs overhead, but what the hell.

You did what you had to do.

■ ■ ■

Twenty minutes later, Wolf was sitting in the passenger seat of the Benz on the other side of the universe. The *nouveau riche* HafenCity district was originally outside the walls of Hamburg. The then-marshy island was where the city fathers executed pirates like the infamous Klaus Störtebeker back in 1401. Six centuries later, it had become the largest urban redevelopment project in Europe. Today, it housed nothing but new-money types who wore ridiculously large and complicated aviator watches that started at five thousand euros.

Wolf used his blue Polizei Hamburg ID card to form a monster line of yellow powder on the open mahogany-paneled door of the glove compartment. Quantity, not quality, he thought.

He snorted the whole thing in one loud, prolonged go. As the meth flamed down the back of his throat, he shut his eyes and squeezed his nose with thumb and forefinger. When the burning turned into that phlegmy feeling under his tonsils, he rolled down the window and spat it onto the pristine sidewalk.

Towering above his head were rows of luxury condos. Most were made of ugly concrete slabs that cast long moonlight shadows. Most had floor-to-ceiling windows with wide-open curtains that advertised obscene wealth.

In the sixth-floor penthouse at the far end of the street, a punk admired his own reflection in an oversized window and made adjustments to gelled hair that Wolf could almost smell from the street. Two minutes after the punk disappeared from the window, the apartment went dim but not all the way dark. He probably had all kinds of dimmers and timers to match his mood and schedule.

Five minutes later, the overly bright headlights of a Lexus

emerged from the underground garage and cut across the shadows, temporarily blinding Wolf even though he was already sitting low in his seat. He waited until the red brake lights flashed in his side mirror. Then he fired up the Benz, which purred to a start with reassuring calm. He eased the column shifter into gear and made a sweeping U-turn. Once the old diesel had straightened out, he switched on the headlights and started his loose tail.

A series of turns and bridge crossings brought them to the harbor. Wolf adjusted his hands on the wheel and followed his prey into the night.

TWO

Beatdown

The Lexus turned left at Teufelsbrück. Wolf didn't. He knew where the punk was headed. An expensive seafood place on the jetty.

Restaurant Engel was the perfect meeting venue for lowlife gangsters and their enablers in the entertainment industry. Pretentious and expensive. The little prick was probably cutting a movie deal with some "edgy" suit from Studio Hamburg.

Wolf ignored the parking lots on either side of the street. Both would have cameras. He picked a dark, quiet side street and cut the engine under an old oak tree, shielded by a high hedge that was well trimmed.

He got out of the Benz slowly, like a commuter returning home from a long day at the office. He walked to the back of the car, keyed the trunk, grabbed the duffel bag out of the wheel well, and threw it over his shoulder. Then he slammed the trunk, walked back to the front, and locked the driver's door.

The twinkling windows at the top of the hill reminded him of Christmas postcards. Hitching the duffel higher on his shoulder, he turned his back on the picturesque villas and walked with wide steps down the hill toward the glistening harbor.

Even at this distance, he could hear huge steel containers being loaded onto a ship. Each time the cranes slammed down another container, it sounded like a shotgun blast echoing across the Elbe River.

He sniffed a numb nostril and kept walking. He found the Lexus without trouble. It was parked as far away from the lamp posts as possible. The punk probably had a habitual fear of light.

Wolf snapped open his Zippo and fired up a Camel. The front plate matched the number in his head. The hood was still hot to the touch and crackling. The parking lot had nothing but late-model luxury cars.

He trailed cigarette smoke across the long footbridge to the jetty. It was a pleasant night, except for those shotgun blasts. And the scumbags in the restaurant.

He counted one–two–three surveillance cameras pointing in different directions. The dead angle was in the shadows, under the stairs on the harbor side. He took a last hit off his cigarette, pinched the butt, and put it in the side pocket of his jacket. Then he hitched the duffel higher on his shoulder and headed for the shadows.

Behind the stairs, he carefully let the bag down onto the concrete landing. He unzipped a side pocket, pulled out his flask of Jack, unscrewed the top, and took a long pull. It warmed his stomach and made him shudder.

He screwed the top back on. Tonight of all nights, he had to keep a clear head. *You never get a second chance to make a first impression*. He laughed silently and reached for his baggie.

■ ■ ■

Half a dozen lines and twice as many cigarettes later, Wolf heard a commotion above his head. Something was crashing down the steps with painful grunts. Correction: somebody. The poor bastard tried to stop his fall by grabbing the rails, but an oversized shadow kicked him viciously.

Great, Wolf thought. That was all he needed. A guest upstairs calling the cops and ruining his evening. Then he saw the gelled hair. It was the punk, complete with sharkskin suit and too much aftershave. Wolf wanted to laugh. Instead, he moved deeper into the shadows.

A bearded giant had grabbed the punk by the scruff of the neck and was dragging him toward the water. A second thug was cursing at him in a language Wolf didn't understand but recognized as Albanian. A third seemed to be in charge. So the punk was getting knocked around by his own clan.

The first two Albanians began kicking the punk in the ribs, while the third watched. Their feet stayed away from the punk's face. That made this a disciplinary beating ordered by their boss. Wolf grinned. The thugs were doing his work for him.

THREE

It's Starting

"We got a bad one," Motz Beck said as he clomped up to Thomas Ritter's desk. The two homicide detectives shared a large office on the sixth floor of the Polizeipräsidium with Meike Voss, who was out getting computer training.

"How bad?" Ritter said, studying the beefy face above his partner's black FC St. Pauli T-shirt. The deep scar in Motz's grizzled blond buzzcut was dark and pulsing.

"Mustafa Hasani," Motz said. "You know, Sulejman Hasani's nephew."

"Uh-oh," Ritter said. There was very, very bad blood between Motz and the Albanian mafia boss. Especially after their brutal encounter in a rusty cargo container six months earlier. That plus the murder of Motz's former partner got Sulejman Hasani a life sentence with zero possibility of parole.

"It's starting," Motz said.

Ritter nodded. With Sulejman Hasani locked up in Santa Fu, the family business must have gone to shit. Now the sharks were circling. Everybody wanted a piece of the clan's heroin trade.

"Cause of death?" Ritter said.

"Shotgun blast to the face," Motz said with unblinking brown eyes.

"Ouch," Ritter said. "That must have really smarted."

That got a momentary grin out of Motz.

Ritter wondered what he was really thinking. The gashes from the overhead handcuffs had become pink scars under his hairy wrists. But Ritter knew from combat that the drenched-sheet shakes came after the actual ordeal. And Motz had just gotten pulled back into his own real-life nightmare.

"Where'd Mustafa Hasani get hit?" Ritter said.

"Teufelsbrück," Motz said. "They found him in the parking lot, in the trunk of his car."

"That sounds like an execution," Ritter said.

Motz shrugged. "Hasani's just settling into his new cell. Instead of programming his cable channels and marking his territory like a normal animal, he's spreading his usual mayhem on the outside."

"That's conjecture," Ritter said.

"That's common sense," Motz said. "He's still running things."

Despite his previous line of thought, Ritter agreed. Hasani was pure evil. And he ruled his clan with an iron fist. Even behind bars, he scared the shit out of the criminal element in Hamburg. Civilians had no clue. Maybe the coroner should give public workshops on Hasani torture techniques.

Motz's eyes were grim. Both detectives knew this case wouldn't end well. Wherever you found Hasanis, you could throw out the book.

FOUR

Devil's Bridge

Motz slammed the *Combat Rock* CD into the Blaupunkt player under the dark green dash. After a few cracks and pops, Joe Strummer began screaming "Know Your Rights" from the kick panels.

The hard white-leather bucket seat pressed into Ritter's back as the 1970 Dodge Charger blasted through morning traffic in the emergency lane of the B5. With the window up and the stereo cranked, he could barely hear the wailing siren of the blue light he had just placed on the roof.

The Clash album told Ritter two things. First, the Hasanis were a conversational no-go for Motz. They never talked about what happened that moon-lit night on Steinwerder. Ever.

Second, Motz was channeling Laura Wesselmann, a cop killer they arrested just before they nailed Hasani. Motz always grabbed the cars of recent prey from impound. When Ritter first came to town, Motz was driving a vintage Eldorado taken off a St. Pauli pimp. Now he was driving Laura Wesselmann's beautifully restored muscle car. Ritter knew by now this wasn't a game. It went against what he'd been taught in psychology courses, but Motz tried to learn from the scum he put away. It was like profiling in reverse.

Ritter was jolted to the present when the Charger made a wide smoking brodie onto Elbchaussee, fishtailing back into its lane just in time to avoid a head-on with a black Mercedes on the water side of the street. Down below was the Fischmarkt, where Ritter, Motz, and Meike always had their private debriefings.

On the right, the grunginess of the Altona district gave way to Ottensen and Othmarschen, with their two-thousand-euro strollers, aging hipster parents, and overpriced beach clubs along the Elbe River. The sand narrowed to nothing at Flottbek.

In the distance was a long white footbridge out to a white jetty named Teufelsbrück, or "Devil's Bridge," where boats from the mainland ferried commuters to the Airbus plant on Finkenwerder, a small island on the other side of the Elbe.

And there they were, with their plastic badges dangling from colorful straps around their skinny necks, climbing aboard the Airbus Express like a bunch of lemmings. The world outside the workplace didn't really exist for them. Ritter read somewhere that their employer was also their landlord, supplying choice apartments at bargain basement rates, underscoring their masters-of-the-universe self-image.

The Charger gurgled to a stop just shy of the police line, which was keeping rubberneckers away from the crime scene. As Ritter swung open the wide green door and stepped onto sandy asphalt, a uniformed cop approached the driver's side with an admiring whistle. "Nice ride!" he said to Motz.

"Got it out of impound," Motz said. "Belonged to—"

Ritter cut him off. "What've we got, officer?" They had to stay focused, especially at the beginning of an investigation.

The uniform sobered up immediately. "Commuters spotted a pool of blood under a Lexus in the parking lot," he said, pointing to the car with the open trunk. "Two of them called it in. We've got the tapes if you want to hear. And a lot of footage from their phones."

"Later," Ritter said. That was all they needed. Selfies of civilians contaminating the crime scene.

"Are those the witnesses?" Motz said, pointing to the ferry pulling away from the dock.

"We got their IDs and phone numbers," the uniform said, showing him a notepad.

"Good man," Motz said.

"Show us the trunk," Ritter said.

"Yes, sir," the uniform said, holding up the red-and-white tape so they could enter an area crowded with blue-and-white vehicles and white hooded coveralls.

Motz got to the car trunk first. He stepped back quickly, batting away flies.

Ritter took his place. What he saw reminded him of a village outside Kandahar. The victim had no face, just mushy black goo splattered in all directions. This wasn't an execution—it was obliteration. "The shotgun was overkill," he said.

"It works for me," Motz said, struggling with a pair of latex gloves. "Little shit got what he deserved."

"Let's keep it professional," Ritter said half-heartedly.

Motz spat on the ground next to his boot.

Here we go, Ritter thought.

■ ■ ■

"The victim was beaten and kicked before being shot in the face." The speaker was a fat man with a stubby cigar. He pulled up the blood-splattered silk shirt to show bruises on the victim's chest. "That might indicate ritual execution," he said. "Or even revenge."

Professor Dr. Dr. Rudolf Deichmann was the city–state's coroner. With his gray cardigan sweater, beer gut, and big smile, he looked like your favorite grandfather—until you saw him with a buzz saw in one hand and a human brain in the other. Everybody called him Rudi.

Ritter nodded. "It was a message."

"Closed casket," Motz said, snapping the second glove in place. It didn't quite cover the pink scar.

"We know for sure this is Mustafa Hasani?" Ritter said.

"Yes," Rudi said. "The fingerprints are an exact match."

Ritter nodded again.

"Wasn't he Hasani's courier?" Rudi asked. Cigar smoke wafted over the open trunk.

"Yeah," Motz said. "Hasani's favorite nephew."

"Time of death?" Ritter said. Maybe it was a mistake to bring Motz along. He was living in the past. This was a fresh case. You had to approach each one with fresh eyes. Otherwise, you saw only what you wanted to see.

"About two thirty in the morning," Rudi said.

"Right after closing time," Motz said. He stood up and pointed at a two-story restaurant parked on top of the jetty.

Ritter chided himself for underestimating his partner. Motz was a lot smarter—and faster—than he looked. More than one criminal had paid a high price for making Ritter's mistake.

■ ■ ■

"What're all those things in the blood?" Motz said, pointing at Mustafa Hasani's chest. "They look like candy."

"Rainbow," Rudi said, holding up a bagged pill.

Ritter squinted at the clear plastic bag. The tiny oval inside had all the colors of the rainbow.

"What's Rainbow?" Motz said.

"Rainbow is a perverse concoction of fentanyl, a synthetic downer, and methamphetamine, a synthetic upper, that can lead to heart attacks and coma," Rudi said.

"That sounds like a chemical yo-yo," Motz said.

"Well put, young man."

"How long has this Rainbow been on the market?" Ritter said.

"Five months," Rudi said. "And it's spreading. Europol has reports of it everywhere from Stockholm to Barcelona." A long trail of aromatic smoke illustrated his point.

"Is the manufacturer local?" Ritter said.

"That would be my guess," Rudi replied. "But you're the detectives. I'm just a sawbones." The orange glow of his cigar matched the morning sun behind the sparse but stout white bristles on his big head.

"How's it distributed?" Motz said.

"Well, it's a new version of the classic heroin and cocaine cocktail, the so-called speedball, which can be injected or snorted," Rudi said, knocking white ash onto the asphalt. "Rainbow is different. It's in pill form, which makes it accessible to naïve non-junkies, who overdose easily. We get a couple of them a month. They're calling it the zombie drug."

"Zombie?" Ritter said. He didn't like the sound of that.

"Most overdoses don't kill the victims immediately," Rudi said. "They send them into a coma for weeks or even months until somebody finally pulls the plug. Literally."

"Jesus," Motz said, looking closer at the pills on Mustafa Hasani's bloody chest. He used the tip of a wide gloved finger to bag one himself.

"What's the profile of the victims?" Ritter said. Already, he was sensing a motive.

"Good question," Rudi said. "Almost all are young. Most come from good families in Blankenese, Eppendorf, and Pöseldorf."

"So, somebody is breaking into the upper-class market?" Ritter said. And somebody in that market doesn't like being the target of lowlife drug dealers, he thought.

"Either that, or upper-class kids overdose more easily," Rudi said.

Ritter's mental lapse evaporated. He had to watch that. Don't jump to conclusions, he thought. Always test your premises. "Explain," he said.

"People who take hard drugs on a regular basis build up an immunity to the ingredients." Rudi sounded like he was back in his old lecture hall. "For example, someone who regularly inhales crystal meth would barely notice the amphetamine effects of the compound. Conversely, heroin addicts wouldn't be much affected by the fentanyl." His stubby cigar was back in his wide mouth.

"So," Ritter said, continuing his thought, "somebody selling a drug to rich kids would make serious enemies of their rich parents." Maybe his hunch was right after all.

"That makes psychological sense," Rudi said, "but it's outside my area of expertise." Something dark passed behind his eyes. "As a father and grandfather, I can only say that anybody selling that poison deserves to end up in the trunk of a car on Teufelsbrück."

"Amen to that," Motz said.

"Thanks, Rudi," Ritter said. "We'll take it from here."

■ ■ ■

After Rudi left, Motz surprised Ritter again. "Maybe Mustafa Hasani's missing a face because he crossed his uncle."

"That's speculation," Ritter said. "We need to follow the evidence." Not just your personal history with the Albanians, he thought.

Motz shook his head. "I *am* following the evidence." He held up his bagged Rainbow pill. "Maybe Mustafa was tapping into the ruling-class market while his uncle cooled his heels behind bars. Remember, Sulejman Hasani spent a decade cultivating relations with the Hamburg Senate. Their families live in Pöseldorf villas. He wouldn't like—or tolerate—somebody turning their precious little snowflakes into zombies."

It sounded like Motz was making the argument for Ritter's own hunch.

"Killing the golden goose is bad business, and Hasani is a businessman," Motz continued. "Don't let his cruelty fool you. He's smart and serious. When he hurts people, it's for a reason."

Ritter was amazed. Motz sounded almost sympathetic with the clan boss who'd had him beaten half to death. Maybe Motz was right and Ritter was wrong. Maybe this was just Hasani family business.

"Maybe Hasani made an example of Mustafa to maintain discipline now that he's locked up," Motz concluded.

Ritter nodded. "You may be right. Still, I have a hard time seeing Hasani killing his favorite nephew. Family is everything to the Albanians." Then another thought hit him. "Or maybe other members of the clan aren't so sentimental. Maybe they're making a move on Hasani himself."

"Now you're the one who's speculating," Motz said. He smiled weakly, but his eyes were haunted.

Ritter reminded himself just how deep the wounds went. He would have to keep a close eye on his partner. "Okay," he said. "I'll have Meike check Mustafa Hasani's movements in the past twenty-four hours."

Motz gave him a strange look. "I thought Meike was in a computer class."

"Hacking 101 at the Chaos Computer Club," Ritter said with a fake laugh.

"Got it," Motz said. No laugh.

"You and I can go interview the staff of the restaurant," Ritter said, pointing across the footbridge. From their vantage point, it looked like a long white box with a lot of windows.

"Restaurant Engel," Motz said.

As in "angel," Ritter thought. The names in this town. He pulled out his phone and speed-dialed Meike.

FIVE

Angel's Restaurant

As they reached the top of the bridge, Ritter got a better look at the white wooden structure. Restaurant Engel was perched on a kiosk named Imbiss Luzifer. That put an angel on the devil's shoulder. More too-clever wordplay, he thought.

The restaurant was at the top of a narrow wooden staircase on the back of the building, above a small dock that hosted two small rowboats and a bigger powerboat. The perfect place to deliver drugs in the middle of the night.

"They got security cameras in all the right places," Motz said, clomping up next to him. He pointed to the lens discreetly mounted under the balcony just above their heads.

Twenty wooden steps higher, they spotted another camera pointing toward the parking lot. "Bingo," Motz said. "Guess car theft is a problem." There was no camera pointing toward the speed boat.

Ritter pushed open the front door and stepped onto tastefully rustic oak planks holding up square granite-topped tables. Motz was right behind him. The morning sun streamed through the rows of windows on each side of the narrow structure, washing the entire restaurant with white light that blinded Ritter for a moment.

After he blinked away the brightness, he saw a pretty girl in an ankle-length black apron polishing wine glasses at the bar. Her crooked smile reminded him of Jenny, a one-night stand he met his first night in Hamburg the previous spring. Against his better judgement, that had turned into an on-again, off-again affair. He pushed away the thought and got into character. "Who's in charge here?" he said.

The waitress's smile died. It was replaced by the arrogant look of a thin man in another long apron. "May I help you, sir?" he said in haughty nasal tone. Ritter figured him for the head waiter. He had the impression the waitress didn't like him either.

Ritter held up his ID card and went with a hunch. "Did you have a reservation for a Mustafa Hasani last night?"

The head waiter's narrow nose wrinkled, like it had sniffed something unpleasant. "Excuse me?"

"You know, an oily type," Motz said. "Gelled hair, dark complexion, sharkskin suit, noisy aftershave. Looks like the drug dealer who owns the speed boat out back."

Ritter suppressed a laugh.

"I would have to check the reservation list," the head waiter said to Ritter.

"Really?" Motz said, taking a step toward him. "How many scumbags you get in here a night?"

Ritter held up a hand to stop Motz, pulled out his phone with the other, and held up the file photo of Mustafa Hasani that Meike had sent him in the parking lot. "This refresh your memory?" he said.

"Oh, *that* young man," the head waiter said. "Yes, he was in here last night."

"Of course, you had no idea he was the nephew of the most notorious gangster in town," Motz said.

The head waiter gave Ritter an unpleasantly intimate smile.

"The young man sat at the corner table"—he pointed to the corner table—"with three large, dark men with shaved heads and beards." The adjectives seemed to frighten and excite him, but at least he was talking.

Ritter matched his intimate tone. "Could you identify the other three men?"

Motz pulled out a spiral notepad and ballpoint.

The head waiter jumped back so quickly he almost tripped over a gap in the planks under his feet. "No, sir, definitely not!" Then, in a scared whisper: "They all look alike."

Motz snorted.

Ritter couldn't tell whether it was agreement or disgust. Possibly both. What was clear was that the head waiter was terrified of the men who sat at the table with Mustafa Hasani. That was a small fact that might turn out to have big implications.

Motz leaned into Ritter, bringing a whiff of leather and motor oil with him. "Maybe Hasani's guys are going full jihadi now that he's down for the count in Santa Fu," he said under his breath. "No more real estate, just drugs, prostitution, extortion, terrorism."

Ritter turned back to the head waiter, who was busying himself folding and refolding a white cloth napkin. "Did anything strange happen at the corner table?" he said.

The folding stopped. "They had some kind of argument." Then: "I don't want any trouble."

"Your secret is safe with us," Ritter lied.

The head waiter thanked Ritter by blinking his wet eyes.

"Where are the tapes to the cameras outside?" Motz said.

That was Ritter's next question, but he let it ride.

"You would have to ask the owner," the head waiter said.

Ritter gave him an encouraging look.

"He's in his office downstairs." The head waiter walked to a panel of windows and pointed down to the speed boat. "It's in the storeroom at the end of the dock."

* * *

Ritter and Motz pounded their way back down the wooden steps, hung a sharp right, and quickly walked the length of the dock. Ritter threw open a sliding wooden door, revealing a small warehouse lined with large plastic containers filled with lobsters and crabs that appeared to be alive. In the far corner, light streamed from under a small door, accompanied by a metallic clinking sound.

Ritter strode to the door, threw it open, and saw an older version of Mustafa Hasani looking up at him in alarm. The guy's hand had stopped mid-motion on the mechanical adding machine. There were stacks of paper receipts at his elbow.

"You the owner?" Ritter said, stepping up to the desk.

"Who the hell are you?" the guy said, looking back and forth between Ritter and Motz.

"Polizei Hamburg," Ritter said, pulling out his ID card again. "Where are the tapes to the cameras?"

"You have a warrant?" the owner said, regaining his composure.

Motz brushed past Ritter and cleared the desk with a leather-clad arm. The adding machine and phone crashed to the concrete floor. The receipts floated down after them. "That's your warrant," he said.

The owner jumped back from the desk. His swivel chair crashed into the wooden wall behind him.

"You didn't even ask what this is about," Ritter said. The owner looked like somebody who would do "errands" for the Hasanis.

"What *is* this about?" the owner said. "Other than you roughing me up."

"You think that was rough?" Motz said, kicking aside a stainless trash can. Wadded-up paper joined the adding machine, phone, and receipts on the floor.

"Murder," Ritter said. "Right outside your restaurant, last night, right after closing time. Didn't you hear anything?"

"Murder?" the owner stuttered.

"You didn't hear a shotgun blast?" Ritter said, leaning into the table.

The owner backed up against the wall. "The containers across the Elbe sound like shotgun blasts. We hear them all the time."

Ritter had to admit he was right about that. A month earlier, at the height of a surprisingly hot summer, Jenny had taken him to a beach club on the Elbe River in the middle of the night. He had re-holstered his gun only after she told him about the containers, but the alarm bell in his head took the romance out of the night.

"Where are the tapes?" Motz said, reaching for an overhead cabinet two quick steps from the desk.

"You can't—" the owner said.

Ritter blocked him. "Yes, we can."

Motz ripped open the cabinet. Three monitors stared back. "You have three cameras?"

"Yes," the owner said around Ritter. "One for the stairs, one for the front dock, one for the parking lot."

Motz started yanking out tapes. "These them?"

"Yes," the owner said. "I was just about to replace them."

"Show us last night," Ritter said. "Two o'clock."

"But—" the owner said.

"How much are you paying the Hasanis for protection?" Motz said.

Again, Ritter was annoyed—and impressed—by the preemption.

"I–I don't know what you're talking about," the owner said.

"Of course you don't," Motz said, giving Ritter a look. "You just want to keep your face."

■ ■ ■

The first tape showed Mustafa Hasani leaving the restaurant just before two in the morning, three bearded thugs right behind him. One seemed to push him down the stairs. Or he tripped. Hard to tell from that angle.

Motz turned to Ritter, who nodded. It was Hasani's enforcer alright, his second in command, the guy who had taken over the day-to-day family business while his boss was in prison.

The second tape showed the other two bearded animals dragging Mustafa out to the dock, where they yelled at him silently and hit him repeatedly. Mustafa fell to the ground and went into a fetal position. The animals kicked him, while the enforcer watched. When they were done, they dragged him off camera.

In the corner of the frame, Ritter saw something glow, like a cigarette. "Stop!" he said. Maybe they had a witness on tape.

Motz hit a button and the glow stayed in place.

Ritter turned to the desk. "Is there any way to get a close-up?"

"Of course not," the owner said. "It's just a surveillance camera."

Ritter made a mental note to have Forensics get them a hi-res print of the shot. He nodded to Motz again.

Motz switched back to the first tape and fast forwarded to the time just before the attack on the second tape. The camera suddenly moved away from the parking lot. "Somebody tampered with it," he said. "Looks like the Albanians knew what they were doing."

Ritter felt a familiar tingling at the base of his skull. The thugs hadn't bothered with the camera on the dock recording the brutal assault, but they did move the camera that would have filmed the murder itself. "I think it's time we paid Hasani's troops a visit," he said. "You okay with that?"

"More than okay," Motz said, an ugly look in his brown eyes. "Got some unfinished business with them."

"Hope you don't have anything reckless in mind," Ritter said, not believing his own words.

"Wouldn't do anything you wouldn't do," Motz said with a mean grin that matched the coldness in his eyes.

Ritter winced at the memory. The rat squad had ruled his killing of Hasani's bodyguard a good shooting, but he and Motz knew it was an execution.

PETER SARDA

SIX

We're the Law

The Charger bumped over the curb, across the wide sidewalk, and up to Casino Esplanade, scattering pedestrians in slow motion.

Ritter looked over at his partner. Motz had a grim look on his face. The two detectives had hardly exchanged a word on the ride down here. Both were lost in thought. The last time Motz was here, he had walked into a deadly trap.

Ritter was halfway out of the car before it completely stopped. He knew he had to lead on this one. Motz was unpredictable even under normal circumstances. This was not a normal circumstance.

Ritter walked quickly to the double doors sandwiched between two massive stone pillars. In the brass-framed glass, he saw Motz strapping a snub-nosed .38 onto his ankle. Ritter could only imagine what was going through his head.

When Motz finally clomped up, Ritter pulled open the right door of the casino and badged the first bearded guard. Over his shoulder, he saw Motz bump the guard hard and kick through the turnstile.

At the elevator, Ritter said, "Sure you're okay?"

"Never felt better," Motz said. He pulled out and cocked his P6.

The gamblers at the roulette table gasped.

The elevator dinged open. Ritter got in and held the doors.

Motz reholstered his gun and stepped aboard, making the elevator sag for a moment. The doors rolled shut silently.

"Want me to play good cop?" Motz said.

Ritter laughed. At least Motz hadn't lost his sense of humor. "Works for me," he said and hit 3.

The elevator whooshed them upward. The glass walls made the smooth movement unpleasant to think about.

The doors dinged open again at the third floor. The two detectives marched into the large room, past the blackjack table, and over to the red carpeted stairs, Ritter in the lead. He took the stairs two at a time, his hand near his holster. The thick carpet cushioned his footsteps.

At the landing, Ritter was greeted by a silent, hostile guard a head taller than he was. The bearded giant's muscles were straining the seams of his jacket. The shiny fabric had an ugly bulge under the left arm.

Motz huffed up the last two steps.

Ritter shoved his ID card into the giant's face. Without stopping, he banged on the door with his other fist. Nothing. He pocketed the card, took two steps back, and prepared to kick the lock free from the doorframe.

The door opened on its own. The giant looked inside.

Ritter used his mistake against him, kicking the back of his knee just hard enough to get him moving. As the giant stumbled into the room, Ritter propelled him forward with more directed kicks until he was facing a bank of windows overlooking Gustav Mahler Park.

This time, Ritter put all his weight into the kick. The giant had a hard landing.

Ritter counted two more bearded Albanians with shaved heads. "You in charge?" Ritter said to the one rising from behind the desk. His prison stare matched the file photo of Hasani's enforcer—and the surveillance video from Restaurant Engel.

The third Albanian pounded carpet toward Ritter.

Motz slammed the butt of his P6 into the guy's skull. The semi-giant went down harder than Ritter's giant. He didn't move after that. Motz looked around wildly, but no more Hasanis appeared.

"I know you, Herr Kommissar," the enforcer said to Motz, his tit muscles flexing under his too-shiny suit. His beady eyes were laughing.

"I know you too," Motz said, moving toward the desk. "And I know where you live."

Ritter stepped between them. "We have you on video," he said to the enforcer.

"Who are you?" the enforcer said, his eyes still on Motz.

"We're the law," Motz said. "Wanna see our badges?" He held up his gun and waved it in the enforcer's face.

Ritter's giant made a move to get up.

"Sit!" Ritter yelled. When the giant hesitated, Ritter took two quick steps toward him, preparing another kick.

The giant looked at his unconscious partner on the ground and went limp.

"We're here about Mustafa Hasani," Ritter said, turning back to the enforcer.

"Mustafa isn't here," the enforcer said.

"No, Mustafa isn't here," Motz said. "Mustafa isn't anywhere." His left eye was twitching.

The enforcer finally looked at Ritter. "Your partner is talking crazy. Maybe somebody hit him too hard in the head."

Motz aimed the square barrel of his gun at the shaved head. The twitching in his eye went into overdrive.

"Mustafa is dead," Ritter said.

The enforcer's eyes went wide.

Aha, Ritter thought. Hasani's enforcer really didn't know about Mustafa. Albanian gangsters couldn't fake surprise. It wasn't part of their acting repertoire.

. . .

"Where were you last night between midnight and three in the morning?" Ritter repeated.

"I was in a meeting with my associates," the enforcer said, gesturing toward the two thugs on the ground. Ritter's giant was sitting obediently on his ass. Motz's semi-giant was moaning his way back to consciousness.

"You call kicking the living shit out of somebody a meeting?" Motz said.

Ritter ignored him. "I said *where*." He felt Motz relax.

"At a restaurant," the enforcer said.

"The restaurant have a name?" Ritter said.

"Engel. You know, like heaven." The enforcer was getting his attitude back.

"Or Teufelsbrück," Motz said. "Like hell." His gun was back in business, this time aimed at the enforcer's stomach.

"Witnesses?" Ritter said uneasily. Motz's fear and anger were effective interrogation tools—as long as they didn't prompt him to pull the trigger. The last thing they needed right now was a police-involved shooting justified with the throw-down gun on Motz's ankle.

"My business associates," the enforcer said. He motioned to the two thugs again, but his eyes were on Motz's gun.

"Mustafa a business associate?" Ritter said.

The enforcer frowned. "He is more of a business *assistant*," he said finally, grinning at his thugs like he'd made a good joke.

Motz's thug ventured a half-hearted smile.

Motz's gun stopped the smile.

"You kill him?" Ritter said.

"What!" the enforcer said.

"You heard me," Ritter said, moving swiftly to the other side of the desk. He was now close enough to strike.

The enforcer looked confused. Hasani obviously hadn't hired him for his brains. "Why would I do that?" he said. "Mustafa is the boss's favorite nephew."

"The boss wouldn't recognize Mustafa now," Motz said. "Somebody shot his face off." He paused. "You that somebody?"

The enforcer's eyes blazed. "You can't pin that on me, Herr Kommissar!"

"We can do whatever we want," Motz said.

"We have you on video," Ritter reminded the enforcer. "Beating and kicking your so-called business assistant."

"Wonder what the boss would think of that?" Motz said.

"Oh, that," the enforcer said dismissively. But his furrowed brow told Ritter he was worried about Hasani's wrath. "We just had a little misunderstanding."

"You call beating a man half to death a little misunderstanding?" Ritter said.

Motz winced.

Ritter regretted his choice of words. He had just described his partner's own ordeal in the container.

"Where we come from, obedience is very important," the enforcer said solemnly. "You people don't understand."

"Where we come from—the German soil you're standing on—revenge is very, very important," Motz said.

Ritter held up his hand. "So, you admit to killing Mustafa Hasani."

"No, no," the enforcer said, backing into the bank of windows. "I had nothing to do with that."

"What about your buddies?" Motz said in a voice that had

moved away. He was addressing the thugs on the ground. "You two kill the boss's favorite nephew?"

The thugs stared at the ground in silence.

Ritter took out a bundle of plastic cuffs. "Looks like we have to take you gentlemen into custody."

"You can't do that!" the enforcer said.

"You're right," Motz said. "Our hands are full." He waved his gun again. "You get to do the honors."

■ ■ ■

After the enforcer cuffed his associates, Motz holstered his gun and did the same to the enforcer's ape-like wrists, pulling the plastic extra tight. "See how easy that was?" he said. "One hand cuffs the other."

Ritter allowed himself a grin.

The enforcer turned his wide shoulders to face Motz, whose hand went back to his holster. "Nice scar, Herr Kommissar," the enforcer said. He pointed to Motz's forehead with his own shiny skull. "Get that on Steinwerder?"

The butt of Motz's gun smashed viciously across the enforcer's face. Once. Twice. Three times. Blood sprayed the wide windows behind him, an abstract painting on top of the leafy still life outside.

Ritter's grin grew. He couldn't have done better himself.

The enforcer's nose was mush, one cheekbone was caved in, and there was a deep gash in the other. He crumpled over, groaning in pain.

Motz used his motorcycle boot to push him onto his face. Then he cuffed his ankles to his wrists. The result looked like a pig about to be roasted over a fire. A pool of blood grew around the pig's face.

Ritter's grin was beginning to hurt. He turned away from the blood and called in a van to pick up the suspects. He told the dispatcher that all three murder suspects had resisted arrest. He didn't order an ambulance.

SEVEN

King's Gambit

Sulejman Hasani pressed the handkerchief to his nose and moved the black pawn to f4, tempting the white pawn on e5 to take it. If white accepted the challenge, he would play d4 and Bxf4, regaining the central gambit with central domination.

Hasani first read about the King's Gambit in *Chess Life* as a schoolboy in the People's Socialist Republic of Albania. Boris Spassky had just used it to beat Bobby Fischer in the World Chess Championship. Hasani had been perfecting the game ever since.

His current opponent was sitting in a wheelchair, paralyzed from the waist down, thanks to the infidel Ritter. Until that fateful night on Steinwerder, Hasani had been a free man, and the paraplegic across from him had been his favorite bodyguard. Now Hasani had the privilege of emptying his cellmate's colostomy bag in their shared stainless-steel toilet.

At least the guards kept the door open most of the time. That—plus protection—cost Hasani a thousand euros a month, but it was well worth it. The last thing he wanted was a fatal power-tool "accident" in the woodshop.

After his cellmate took the black pawn, Hasani noted the color of the fluid on his handkerchief. Pale yellow this time. He sighed. Probably the beginning of yet another infection. He would have to get more antibiotics from the infirmary, just in case. He flipped the handkerchief over to the clean side and moved the next black pawn up to d4.

He felt eyes on him. Reflexively, he dropped the handkerchief and clutched the handle of the homemade shank in his sleeve.

He relaxed his grip when he saw it was his less favorite bodyguards. Both were alumni of Steinwerder. Both had received nontrivial injuries at the hands of Ritter. But the neck braces had come off long before their trials. Now both had worried looks on their faces.

Hasani waved them in. "What is it?" he said impatiently, his mind drifting back to Bxf4. This had better be good.

After hesitating too long, the first bodyguard cleared his throat and plunged in. "Hells Angels selling something new out of E Block." He held up a colorful pill.

Hasani stiffened at the mention of his new archenemies. Willi Kaiser's biggest muscle on the outside was Hasani's biggest threat on the inside. His first week in Santa Fu, their neo-Nazi leader, a very large and heavily tattooed animal named Preacher sent a couple of goons to "invite" Hasani to a "Come to Jesus" meeting. Hasani doubted the devil worshippers had their own clergy. It was probably just a satanical word game meant to confuse the uninitiated.

At the appointed time and place—noon in an empty shower room with drippy faucets, moldy tiles, and the smell of industrial cleanser—Preacher appeared in a black robe that showed off his immense bulk and a very dirty clerical collar that choked the thick neck below his thick shaved head.

Preacher laid down the law. "Render unto Caesar the things that are Caesar's and unto God the things that are God's." He underlined his point by showing Hasani two oversized fists. The fingers of the right fist were tattooed "GOOD," the fingers of the left "EVIL." Preacher bumped them together a couple of times, like some kind of spiritual struggle. It was a silly threat, but a real one.

By Preacher's moronic logic, Hasani owed him the same monthly protection money he paid the prison guards. The first payment was due the following day.

Hasani decided that Preacher was schizophrenic, probably the result of taking too many of his own drugs. But that just made him more dangerous.

Hasani brushed back the memory and squinted at the multi-colored pill between his bodyguard's grubby thumb and forefinger. It looked like candy for schoolgirls. "What is that?" he said, reaching for a fresh handkerchief. The one on the ground would have to be thoroughly cleansed with antiviral disinfectant.

"They call it Rainbow," the bodyguard said.

"How creative," Hasani said.

"Should we do something about it?" his partner asked.

Hasani shook his head. "As I keep telling you, we do not sell narcotics in here. We play the long game."

Both bodyguards assumed parade rest, their heads bowed, their hands crossed respectfully at the groin.

"Now that Innensenator Mertens is out of the way, our friends in the Hamburg Senate are moving ahead to buy up more and more of St. Pauli," Hasani explained. "They are moving a little slower than we had hoped, given our recent cash flow problem." He cautiously sniffed the handkerchief. It smelled fresh enough. "But real estate, not drugs, is the future."

"What about the next shipment of Afghan Gold?" the first bodyguard asked.

In a split second, Hasani was at his throat with the razor-sharp shiv. "Silence!" he hissed. "The walls in here have ears."

The bodyguard looked straight ahead, aware that his life hung by a thread. His partner did the same.

Hasani felt another set of eyes. Without removing the knife from the bodyguard's throat, he looked to the doorway with annoyance. "What is it?" he said. Nothing but interruptions this morning.

"You've got a visitor," the prison guard said. He looked at the ground instead of the knife.

"I'll be right there," Hasani said.

After the guard left, Hasani turned back to his hapless underling. "Remember what I told you." Then he released him. "And watch over our brother while I am gone," he ordered, nodding toward his chairbound cellmate, who was staring at d4 morosely. He obviously suspected a trap.

EIGHT
Visiting Day

Kriminalhauptkommissar Wolf took a deep drag on his Camel and looked to the door impatiently. This early in the morning, he was the only guest in the large visiting room, which contained a dozen tables, each with two chairs.

The prison guard had told him there was no smoking in Santa Fu, but the rules were flexible, to say the least. Two hundred euro bills taken off a loser drug dealer in St. Pauli had gotten him a special audience with special privileges. Wolf dropped the cigarette onto the polished concrete floor, ground it out with his boot, and reached for the pack in the side pocket of his sports jacket.

There was some commotion at the door. The guard led an old man into the room. Sulejman Hasani had aged a lot since his trial. He was holding a white handkerchief to his left nostril. Wolf wondered how much he was paying for protection.

Hasani looked around the room in irritation. "Where is my nephew?" he asked the guard in a surprisingly high voice.

"You have another guest," the guard said, gesturing at Wolf.

"Who the hell is that?" Hasani said, backing toward the door. His eyes looked wary.

"Polizei Hamburg," Wolf said. "Your friend and helper." He shook loose a fresh cigarette, grabbed it with his teeth, fired it up, and snapped his Zippo shut. Smoke rings wafted up to the fire extinguishers bolted to the ceiling. It looked like they had been painted over more than once.

Hasani turned to leave. "I do not talk to the police," he said.

"No problem," Wolf said agreeably. "I'll do the talking for both of us."

Hasani gave him a look that was supposed to chill his bones.

Wolf laughed. "Take a load off," he said, pointing to the empty chair across from him. "Or do you have a scheduling conflict with your manicurist in C Block?" He spat a stray piece of tobacco onto the concrete.

"What do you want?" Hasani said, studying his handkerchief.

"That's the wrong question," Wolf said. "The right question is: What do I have?"

Hasani trained his hot black eyes on Wolf again.

"C'mon in, big guy," Wolf said. "Make yourself at home. Or do you want the whole world to hear your secrets?"

Something in Hasani's eyes changed. He waved the guard away.

The door banged shut. The lock turned over twice.

Hasani made his way to the table slowly, like someone entering a sick room.

"See, that wasn't so hard, was it?" Wolf said.

Hasani stopped. "Who the hell are you?"

"Your new friend."

"I do not have new friends, only old friends."

Wolf nodded, like Hasani had agreed with him. Then he put a sad look on his face. "I'm afraid I've got some bad news," he said. "Please, sit down." He gestured to the chair again.

Hasani didn't move a muscle.

Wolf sighed. "It's about your nephew," he said. "Mustafa."

"What about Mustafa?" Hasani said. "Why is he not here?"

"Yeah, I know," Wolf said. "Today is visiting day. That makes this especially hard."

Hasani took a step closer, reaching into his sleeve. "That makes what hard?"

Wolf flicked his half-smoked cigarette at the gangster and reached for his ankle holster.

Hasani jumped back, brushing sparking ash off his coveralls.

Wolf came up with his second gun, the one he hadn't placed in the sliding tray at the bulletproof sign-in window. He slammed the .38 onto the table, the short barrel pointing at Hasani's midsection. "That shank up your sleeve won't do you any good," he said, fingering the trigger. The print-resistant tape felt good against his palm.

Hasani held out empty hands for him to see.

"That's better," Wolf said. "I think we understand each other now."

"Where is Mustafa?" Hasani said. His eyes looked concerned now.

"Oh, him," Wolf said. "You don't need to worry about Mustafa."

"Where is he?"

Wolf sighed loudly. "Mustafa is at the morgue," he said. "You might have trouble identifying him. His face is missing."

Hasani's eyelids flickered once. But that was it. Nothing else moved.

"Yes, I know," Wolf said, the picture of understanding. "This must come as a big shock to you. Would you like a glass of water? A smoke maybe?" He held up the pack and shook loose another cigarette.

Hatred appeared in Hasani's eyes.

"No?" Wolf shrugged. "Oh, right, you don't smoke. It's against your religion or something. I can respect that." He paused. "You don't mind if I indulge, do you?"

Hasani seemed to be looking at something behind Wolf's head. Probably his grave.

"I'll take that as a yes," Wolf said. He squinted against the big flame and then snapped the Zippo shut. "Ah," he said, exhaling another dose of nicotine.

"Why should I believe you?" Hasani said. "I do not know you."

Wolf laughed smoke. "Good question," he said, reaching into the pocket of his jacket with his free hand. He pulled out a glossy of Mustafa, or what was left of him, and slammed it onto the table next to the gun. "Doesn't do him justice, I know," Wolf said. "They say he was a cute kid. Hard to tell now with all that muck where his face should be."

Hasani's eyes took in the photo but didn't give anything away. Either he wasn't really all that close to his nephew or he had an iron will, one of those guys who revealed nothing to the enemy.

Wolf figured both. "Thing is," he continued, "you've got to be asking yourself: Who did this? And why?" He took another drag on his cigarette. "At least that's what I'd be asking in your shoes."

Hasani's eyes had a shade of respect that wasn't there before.

"I think you know me now," Wolf said, putting the photo back in his pocket.

Hasani nodded almost imperceptibly.

"That leads us to the next question," Wolf said. "It's almost metaphysical. What's the price of truth?"

"You tell me," Hasani said sullenly.

"How about fifty grand?" Wolf said. "If you aren't satisfied with the answer, I'll give you your money back, no questions asked. Cross my heart and hope to die."

Hasani's eyes hardened.

"Okay, okay," Wolf said, throwing up a hand. "I shouldn't joke about a thing like that." His other hand remained on the gun.

"Who is responsible?" Hasani said.

Wolf nodded earnestly and sat forward in his chair. "My sources tell me it was the Hells Angels."

"Why would a motorcycle gang kill my nephew?" Hasani said.

"That's another good question," Wolf said. "I'll throw in the answer for free. They're going after you."

Hasani smiled coldly. "They are going after me? By killing my nephew?"

"Well, it's not so much the Hells Angels as their employer."

"Their employer?"

"An old friend of yours," Wolf said. "So to speak."

"What old friend?" Hasani had an ugly look on his face.

"Willi Kaiser," Wolf said slowly, enunciating each syllable.

Hasani's face went dark. He seemed to be looking inside himself.

"Yeah, I know," Wolf said, enjoying the effect the name had on him. "It's hard to believe, isn't it? Now that you're here behind bars, your big enemy, Willi Kaiser, is making a move on you. Who would have thought it?"

"Why should I believe you?" Hasani said.

Wolf grinned. "Trust me, I'm a police officer."

Hasani glared at him.

"But seriously, Sulejman," Wolf said. "I *can* call you by your first name, can't I? I mean, now that we're new friends."

The glare hardened.

"Okay, okay," Wolf said. "Maybe I was a bit premature with that. I mean, we only just met. What would people say?"

"What makes you think that Kaiser is responsible?" Hasani said.

"Now we're getting somewhere," Wolf said. "*Kaiser is responsible.* I like that."

"How!" Hasani yelled.

Wolf twisted his lips. "A little birdie told me."

Hasani moved quickly for a man his age.

Wolf felt the blade graze his chin as he jumped back from the table, the .38 shaking in his hand. His chair crashed loudly behind him.

The guard appeared at the door.

Wolf shook his head without taking his eyes off Hasani. I have this under control.

The guard closed and locked the door again.

"Drop it," Wolf said to Hasani, cocking the .38 while keeping it trained on the gangster's nose. "Now."

Something metallic clattered on concrete.

Wolf stepped around the table, waving Hasani back with the gun, scooped up the prison knife, and dropped it into his pocket next to the photo. Then he waved Hasani to the upright chair. "Sit," he said.

Hasani did as he was told.

"So," Wolf said. "What we've got here is a situation."

Hasani stared at the table.

"I know who killed your nephew," Wolf continued. "You obviously want revenge."

Hasani looked up in surprise.

"Everything has a price," Wolf said. "Truth has a price. Revenge has a price. Friendship has a price."

Respect appeared in Hasani's eyes again. "What is your name?" he said.

Wolf slapped a business card onto the table. It had a blue Polizei Hamburg logo.

Hasani picked it up. "Kriminalhauptkommissar Wolf," he read out loud. "LKA 68. Narcotics Division." He turned the card over, found nothing, and turned it back.

Wolf laughed. "You can call me Mister Wolf, if you want."

"Okay, Mister Wolf," Hasani said. "What is your price?"

"Now you're talking," Wolf said. "Let's make a deal." The gun was still in his hand, but it was at his side. "How about we stick with round numbers? Say, a hundred grand? I'll even forget the fifty grand finder's fee. Whaddya think?"

Hasani nodded.

"Okaaay," Wolf said. "It looks like we got ourselves a deal." Then he grinned sheepishly. "You'll forgive me if I don't shake on it. I mean, God only knows what other weapons you have on you."

Hasani smiled slightly.

"That leaves just one other question," Wolf said.

Hasani's smile froze.

"Who pays?"

"I will see that you are paid." Hasani sounded irritated.

"No, no," Wolf said. "That's not what I mean. What I mean is, who pays for Mustafa?"

"You said Kaiser is responsible," Hasani said.

"Indirectly, yes," Wolf said. "Technically, he's the boss of bosses. But the actual order came from further down the chain of command."

"Who ordered the hit?"

"My sources tell me it was Lutz Kopperschmidt. The president of the Hells Angels."

"Lutz Kopperschmidt," Hasani said, like he knew the name. "His people are spreading their dirty drugs in this cesspool. They have a captive market." There was a hint of admiration in his voice.

"I see," Wolf said.

"Lutz Kopperschmidt sent a message," Hasani said. "I would have done the same."

"A message?" Wolf wanted to laugh. Crime bosses always tried to sound poetic about their mayhem.

"Mustafa was a message," Hasani explained.

"Yeah, I got that part," Wolf said. Enough of this haiku shit, he thought. "What do you want to do about it?"

"I want to send a counter message."

"Care to be more specific?"

"Who is closest to Lutz Kopperschmidt?" Hasani said. "He must have a nephew."

"No, he doesn't," Wolf said. "Just a half-brother named Mikey. He could be Lutz's son. They have the same father but different mothers."

"Find him."

"And then what?" Wolf said. "Just to be clear."

"What do you think?"

Wolf grinned. "I'm just funning you," he said. "I'll get right on it." He knocked on the table twice and sauntered away, his gun hand away from the gangster. "Door!" he yelled to the guard.

The bolt turned in the lock.

Wolf looked back at Hasani. "See you in church," he said.

NINE

Safe House

After crossing the bridge from Denmark, the black van made good time. The Autobahn was relatively free this early in the morning.

The two federal agents in front listened to *Schlager* hits on the radio, while the two young, uniformed cops in back fought yawns and checked their phones for the umpteenth time. Their "guest" was strapped into a specially designed seat facing them.

"I gotta take a mean piss," Laura Wesselmann said. She squirmed in the seat, but the cuffs and harness kept her in place.

"Hold it," the BKA guy said from behind her head. "We're almost there."

Laura stared at the uniformed breeder cop facing her but spoke to the federal agent up front. "I ain't kidding."

Actually, she was. She had a strong bladder and no Astra beer for the past six months, so she didn't feel a twinge, even after four hours on the road. She just wanted to rub her wrists and stretch her legs. And maybe make her getaway.

"Life's a bitch," the BKA guy said.

Laura looked up at her left hand, just hanging there, like it belonged to somebody else. Twenty minutes after being cuffed to the overhead rail, it went to sleep. Now it didn't tingle anymore.

It was just gone.

Goddamn BKA fucks weren't taking any chances. Probably warned by that Ritter asshole.

Laura already missed the Danish cops, even if they did shoot Konny to bits on that meth farm. At least they didn't chain her up like a monkey. Besides, Konny hadn't given them much choice, blazing away with her sawed-off shotgun like that. Of course, the Hells Angels blamed Laura for leading the cops to the lab, so she *had* to rat them out.

Now every Death Head in Northern Europe was gunning for her, especially the Hamburg Chapter. They owed Copenhagen because they'd set up the meet with Konny and, by extension, Laura. Talk about too many cooks.

All Laura had wanted was to get the fuck out of Hamburg. Preferably on a cargo ship headed for a tropical island without an extradition treaty. Instead, she got perp-walked in a Europol raid thought up by Ritter.

So now here she was, sitting in an "unmarked" police van that wasn't shit compared to Konny's Dodge Ram—no sunroof, no smoked glass, no Clash, no crank—headed for a "safe house." She, the baddest bad girl of them all. It was crazy.

Laura shifted her position and examined the uniformed girl cop. Small, like Laura, with long braided blonde hair, she looked hot to trot.

Out Heidi's window, the first signs of civilization flew by. The big blue one with all the arrows said Hamburg was only thirty kilometers away. Shit. They were driving her back into Ritter territory.

Laura yanked on the handcuff again. It was a stupid reflex, but what the fuck, you never knew. Her dead hand just bounced around like a rubber Halloween prop.

That got a smirk from the breeder.

Fuck him too. Laura visualized putting her right heel through his oinker and sending the bone into his pea brain.

Something clinked beneath her.

The shackles on her ankles would fuck up that plan—or make it better. After crushing the breeder's nose, she could strangle him with the chains. Like Konny said, *Luck is just another name for Plan B*. Laura cackled.

The breeder didn't like that.

Laura was thrown against the sliding door by a sharp turn. After righting herself, she saw that everything outside was wrong. Instead of heading into the city, the van had taken another turn and was going deeper into the woods. With growing alarm, she saw a sign that said "*Naturschutzgebiet*." Nature conservation area. What the fuck?

She halfway wondered if the BKA guys were going to bury her ass behind a tree. Then she remembered Heidi. Nope. Too many witnesses. And not enough balls in the van. Herself excluded. She cackled again.

After more bouncing on another back-ass road, sharp rays of sunlight punctured the unsmoked windows, blinding her. At least they were out of the woods.

The van slowed at a sign. "Bergstedt." Fuck me, Laura thought. Not another goddamn campsite. She had enough of that shit in Denmark. To her semi-relief, shithole houses bounced by her window. Squaresville beat tree huggers.

Just past a cemetery—how fucking fitting—the van turned into a non-street with a creepy crawler house at the end covered with ivy. Yuck City.

The van stopped in front. This must be it. Home sweet home. Maybe she'd die of boredom with all that nothing around her. At least that would get her out of the trial.

PETER SARDA

TEN

Animal Shelter

The sun was directly overhead, cushioned with fluffy white clouds in a bright blue sky. The perfect day made Wolf want to puke.

He squinted over his Camel and eased the brown Mercedes up over the rounded curb onto the wide sidewalk, halfway blocking a driveway with a post in the middle. He did a quick scan of all the hipsters in wannabe worker clothing taking their lunch breaks in the outdoor restaurants along Neuer Pferdemarkt. Most came from ad agencies and graphic design firms that rented expensive office space in former factory buildings on Schulterblatt, just around the corner. Most had no idea that they were sunning their Carhartt watch caps, lumberjack coats, and carefully oiled beards in former Hells Angels territory. Their female coworkers wore colorful designer eyewear big and clunky enough to house bottle glass.

Lutz Kopperschmidt was sitting on a woven rattan sofa with tasteful gray cushions outside an Italian restaurant. Organized Crime said it was a money-laundering operation for Willi Kaiser, Lutz's *de facto* boss. The president of the Hells Angels had short-cropped black hair gelled to attention, aviator glasses with yellow lenses, and a baby blue golf shirt with the collar up under a golf sweater of a slightly darker hue that clung to a flabby midsection.

He was reading from an expensive-looking tablet computer.

Wolf shook his head and cut the engine. Sure, the Hells Angels were forbidden from wearing their colors in public, but Lutz was really overdoing it. He didn't look like he could bench-press more than fifty kilos. What the hell was this town coming to?

As Wolf hit the hazard light switch on the bubble-like control panel, his thoughts drifted back to his visit in Santa Fu. The prison was only half an hour from here, but it felt light years away. Maybe that was Lutz's problem. What he really needed was the prison experience. That would man him up, but good. In no time, he'd have an SS tattoo over his left tit and biceps the size of his thighs.

After checking the side mirror for delivery trucks, Wolf swung open the car door into the bike lane, took a final drag off his Camel, and dropped it between the huge round cobblestones. Then he locked up and made his way through crowded tables on a large patio that was filled with warm sunlight, loud laughter, and the smell of lasagna and pizza.

He came to a stop at Lutz's sofa. "Working hard or hardly working?" he said.

Lutz looked up in annoyance. Probably checking his stock portfolio. "Cut yourself shaving?" he said.

Wolf's felt his own chin and came back with dry blood. He grinned. "Just a flesh wound." Lutz had no idea that Hasani had just put out a hit on his half-brother—or that Wolf was the hitter.

"Uh-huh," Lutz said.

Wolf sat down on the sofa across from him. "Damn, these things are comfy," he said. "I guess crime does pay."

Lutz gave him what was supposed to be a hard look.

Wolf was tempted to put a dent in it with his P6 but let it go. He was here on business. "Where's my cut?" he said.

Lutz's eyes went to the black nylon sports bag at his feet.

Wolf snorted at the cordovan penny loafers under his orange corduroy trousers.

"You wanna count it?" Lutz said.

"Nah," Wolf said. "Trust is the basis of every friendship. We *are* friends, aren't we, Lutz?"

"What've you got for me?" Lutz said.

"Was that a yes?" Wolf fired up the next to last cigarette in the pack. He knew there was a machine around the corner, but he waved over a waiter anyway.

"Are you ready to order, sir?" the waiter said with a slight Italian accent.

Wolf knew it was affected. According to police records, the kid was second generation, born and raised in Schnelsen, just like Lutz.

"Two cartons of Camels," Wolf said. "Unfiltered and on the house." He pulled back his jacket just far enough to show the butt of his gun.

"Yes, sir," the waiter said, his fake accent gone. He disappeared in the direction of the kitchen.

"Now, where were we?" Wolf said to Lutz. "Oh yeah, we were talking about friendship."

"What have you got for me?" Lutz said again.

"Righto," Wolf said. "A friend in need is a friend indeed."

Lutz gave him the stare again.

Wolf laughed. "Don't get rough. You're gonna love what I got."

"What?"

"Laura Wesselmann," Wolf said. "You know, the dyke who led Europol to your meth lab in Denmark."

Lutz put down his tablet and leaned forward, his soft belly spreading over corduroy. "You got her?"

"All wrapped up in a big red ribbon," Wolf said. "BKA transferred her to a safe house this morning."

Lutz's blue eyes narrowed. "Where?"

"Bergstedt. Around the corner from an animal shelter. I wrote down the address for you." Squinting against cigarette smoke, Wolf tore off a page from his worn leatherbound notepad.

It was Lutz's turn to laugh. "An animal shelter? That's a good one."

"I knew you'd like it," Wolf said.

Lutz slid the sports bag over to Wolf with a penny loafer.

"It's been real and it's been fun," Wolf said, grabbing the bag. "But it hasn't been real fun."

Lutz just waved. He was already on his phone, probably calling an emergency meeting with his "business partners."

"Here's your takeout, sir," the waiter said. He was holding a large doggie bag.

Wolf flicked his live cigarette into a potted oregano plant and looked inside. Two cartons of Camels. "Just what the doctor ordered," he said.

"Anytime, Herr Kommissar."

ELEVEN

Molotov Madness

Rolling waves landed gently on the fine white sands of the private beach, tingling the base of Laura Wesselmann's skull as filtered sunlight warmed her bare skin. Her eyes closed on their own. A slight breeze brought a hint of Coppertone and something earthier, accompanied by the grinding bump of distant techno that drifted along the eastern coast of Ibiza.

The blissful beginnings of after-lunch love play were overshadowed by the slight rumbling of thunder in the distance. Ibiza didn't normally have storms in peak season, but who cared about a little summer rain?

The rumbling got louder and more insistent. Laura's eyelids shot open. It took her a moment to recognize the bedroom furniture. Shit! The safe house. It had just been a dream. She was wide awake now, her pulse spiking.

She pulled Heidi's sinewy arm off her shoulder, jumped out of bed, and raced to the edge of the window. Moving the blinds just a hair, she saw the gleaming chrome of three hogs in the bright moonlight. They were getting bigger and heading straight at her, lights off.

Laura raced to the desk, grabbed Heidi's holster and backpack off the chair, opened the door quickly enough to feel cold air outside, closed it quietly behind her, and sped to the door on the other side of the kitchen. She flew down the stairs silently, then turned and ran in the direction of the rumbling outside the half-submerged basement.

The rumbling stopped. Heavy footsteps were followed by heavy sloshing against the side of the house. The sharp smell was unmistakable. They were splashing gasoline onto the perimeter of the house. In their place, she would have done the same—before shooting up the place with automatic weapons.

A bent ammo clip flashed in one of the small windows. An AK-47. Laura almost took it as a compliment. The Hells Angels knew who they were dealing with. They were loaded for bear.

Something cracked just to the left of the window. A Zippo. Oh shit. Laura yanked the pistol out of Heidi's holster, aimed it at the ankle of the motorcycle boot outside, and squeezed off her first round. A satisfying scream of agony brought a smile to her face. It died instantly when flames filled the small window.

Laura jumped back and crawled across the dirt floor like a spider. The screaming outside got louder. The fire seemed to be moving back and forth. Laura's smile came back. The stupid Angel fuck was burning to death in his own gasoline.

Windows and wood exploded above her head. She didn't have to see past the flames to know that the other Angels were spraying the house with monster rounds, probably at chest height.

Single pops in between told her the breeder cop in the room down the hall from Heidi had found his own handgun and was returning fire. Good move, Laura thought. Reveal your fucking position to the enemy.

Like clockwork, the AK fire focused on something at the other end of the house. Laura cackled. "Told ya."

She wiped sweat from her brow. It was getting hotter by the second. She had to get the fuck out of here *now*. A quick, careful touch test of the low ceiling told her the floor above her was burning. She had to find another way out.

As the AK fire moved closer again, she followed the flames around the windows to a big shadow the size of a small door. She stubbed her toe on a darker shadow underneath. She felt around with her hand. A short staircase. It must lead to an outside door. She took two crouching steps up and banged the shadow with the heel of her free hand. Wood creaked, but her hand was jarred back by a metallic sound that hurt. Fuck. Padlock.

She retraced her steps and took a couple more for good measure. Then she ran at the stairs. She used the second step to propel her right foot at the shadow, kung-fu style. It budged outward for a second, long enough for her to see a hairline of flame in the middle as she bounced back onto the hard dirt floor. She used the momentum to right herself, her eyes still on the hairline. So there were two doors.

A small shadow on the hairline told her where to aim Heidi's gun. It took two shots to blast the lock, another sidekick to get the right door open.

Laura was met by a wall of flame that singed her right foot, reminding her that she was naked. Frantically, she scrambled back down the steps to the far corner of the half-basement. The ground was rough and wrinkly, like a paint tarp, but at least it cooled her hot foot. Her hands made double sure. Halle-fucking-lujah, she thought. The canvas was stiff, but it would do the job.

After some searching, she found Heidi's gear. She jammed the gun into the thick holster and strapped that onto her bare waist, scraping her hip in the process. Then she threw the pack over her shoulders and cinched it down.

That done, she marched back to the tarp, grabbed a corner off the dirt, kicked underneath until it finally opened up, and somehow managed to get the whole smelly thing over her head.

The heavy canvas made it hard to walk, but she followed the light on the dirt back to the blazing doorway. It felt like the canvas was on fire.

With an animal scream, she ran back up the short steps and through the wall of flame. When she felt thick grass under her feet, she threw herself down and rolled and rolled and rolled until the tangled canvas made it impossible to go on. She was blind, dizzy, and completely out of breath. There was no air inside the tarp.

Oh shit, she thought. Paint tarps were usually covered with old paint and turpentine. She flailed around madly to get out of her homemade trap. If she didn't find the opening soon, she would cook to death in the damned thing. She'd heard the Apaches roasted their captives that way, in buffalo hides.

She flailed around some more, but something held her in place. No matter how hard she struggled, she couldn't move. Then she started rolling again, this time against her will. Fuck. Somebody was pushing her back to the fire! She heard that animal scream again. It was muffled this time.

Just when she thought she would pass out, cold air hit her lungs. She took deep gulps of coldness. She could worry about her attacker once she caught her breath.

Flames replaced darkness. Laura wanted to jump up and run, but a shadow stepped in front of the flames and extended a hand. The shadow had shiny skin and sinewy muscles. Heidi!

Laura reached for the hand, but it was gone, replaced by a Heidi-sized doll dancing grotesquely against the flames. A wet soggy mess sprayed Laura's face. She smelled blood as Heidi's body was ripped to bits by a barking AK.

After a few moments of wet nasty silence, the smoking barrel turned toward Laura slowly, like the big shadow behind it was enjoying himself.

Heidi's gun jumped from the holster into Laura's hand. She squeezed off the remaining rounds at the center of the shadow. AK fire blasted hot over her head as the shadow fell backwards.

Laura kicked off the rest of the tarp and stepped over to her wannabe killer, who was writhing on the ground, his hands clutching the bloody holes in his gut.

Laura smirked at him, released the empty magazine from Heidi's gun onto the grass, grabbed a fresh one from her belt, and slammed that into place, her eyes never leaving the writhing mess at her feet.

She fired one shot into each of the asshole's kneecaps before emptying the clip into his crotch. Her only regret was that she didn't have time to sit down and watch him die.

She reloaded Heidi's gun again, reholstered it, and stepped over to the AK, which was glowing like a breathing animal in the grass. She grabbed it and marched toward the gunfire, which was getting more sporadic.

She made it to the front of the blazing house just in time to see two Angels cross the living room. The stupid fucks were *inside* the house. Bad move. She let the AK rip.

The big window splintered as the first Angel flew away from her like a rag doll. The second turned his big barrel toward her. His body completed the motion without the help of his head, which exploded above the fireplace.

That only left the breeder cop, who was probably on the carpet somewhere crying for Mommy the way those Wehrmacht guys did in *Stalingrad*.

Something cut into Laura's left side. She looked down and laughed. She was still wearing Heidi's holster. When she bent forward to loosen the belt, something cut into her shoulders. The backpack. She laughed again and shook it loose and onto the grass in front of her. "Hi, Mom, I'm home," she said. Her laughter was getting hysterical.

Exploding glass in the kitchen window made her duck and trip over the pack. She scooped it up and headed to the street, where the hogs were parked.

She was greeted by scared-looking neighbors in bathrobes and a single siren that was far off but getting closer. "What's the matter?" she said to the gawkers. "Never seen a live sex show before?" She turned toward the choppers, swinging her beautiful ass at her new audience.

She chose the biggest hog, lashed the backpack to the sissy rail, swung her leg over the seat, and loosened the uncomfortable holster. That done, she put her sore right foot on the pedal and jump-started the beast. The inside of her ankle lost some skin, but it was worth it to see all those breeders trying to cover their brats' eyes.

Something big exploded, sending a huge flame into the sky. Laura's eyes were as wide as her smile. Son of a fucking bitch. Probably the gas heater. It was better than New Year's Eve at the Elbe River.

"*Adios*, losers!" she yelled and blasted away into the night, the black sky glowing with fire.

TWELVE

Blame Game

"I just got a disturbing call from BKA," Inspektionsleiter Ebeling said.

In the distance behind his wide oak desk, a steamboat chugged up the Alster River, trailing puffs of white smoke that blended into fluffy white clouds floating in a bright blue sky. From up here, the world looked simple.

It wasn't.

"Our safe house in Bergstedt was hit early this morning," Ebeling said. He adjusted the off-center knot of his school tie and gave Ritter a cold look.

Ritter was stunned. Bergstedt was where Europol had stashed Laura Wesselmann. "How bad is it?"

"As bad as it gets," Ebeling said. "When local police arrived, they found a smoldering ruin, with three bodies inside and two outside. They also found two motorcycles registered to known members of the Hells Angels."

"Is Laura Wesselmann dead?"

"She's missing," Ebeling said. "Two police officers sacrificed their lives for her. One was burned beyond recognition, but Forensics matched his dental records. The other was stripped of her clothing before being shot to pieces with an AK-47."

"Oh Jesus," Ritter said. "That's awful." In Kandahar, he'd seen what a Kalashnikov could do to a family of seven. Scrawny dogs were chewing on the pieces when GSG-9 arrived.

"No kidding," Ebeling said. "You let a cop killer get away. Now two more of our own are dead."

"What!" Ritter was on his feet now. "That's a flat-out lie!"

Six months before, Ebeling himself had ordered Ritter to let Laura Wesselmann escape so she could lead Europol to a massive meth lab outside Copenhagen. The result was a bloodbath that turned the little psycho into a star witness with a safe house instead of solitary confinement in a maximum-security prison.

Ebeling smiled at his ink blot. "You should make sure you have airtight evidence before making such accusations against a superior officer." He looked up. There was a twinkle in his eye. "Do you have anything tangible to back up your wild claim?"

Ritter wanted to punch him. "Is this what you call plausible deniability?" he said. In Kandahar, his unit had gotten indirect orders to do things that none of the special ops were allowed to talk about to anyone back home. Ever. That was the deal. You do the dirty work for us. If you succeed, you get a medal—behind closed doors. If you fail, we don't know you.

"Don't take it so hard," Ebeling said, showing green teeth. "We all make mistakes. I will do my best to protect you from the blowback on this one."

"No, you won't," Ritter said. "Because it wasn't my mistake. It was yours. I told you it was a bad idea to let her run. Too many moving parts, too many things that could go wrong."

"Yes," Ebeling said to the ink blot again. "I agreed that the— how shall I put it?—special operation involved some inherent risks. But you knew that when you took this job."

Ebeling was right, of course. In their first interview, he had made it clear that he knew damning details about Ritter's dark secret in Frankfurt that he would use against him if push ever came to shove. Push had just come to shove.

"I'm glad we had this little chat," Ebeling said. "Sometimes just talking about things helps."

Ritter smiled bitterly. With Ebeling, it was all about covering his ass all the time. Everybody else was collateral damage, especially his lead detective.

There was a short knock at the door.

Thank you, Jesus, Ritter thought. Anything to get him out of here before he fragged his boss.

"Yes," Ebeling said, his eyes on Ritter.

Meike Voss stuck her head in the door and addressed Ritter. "We've got another body," she said. Her red pigtails danced around a bulky sweater that was doing a poor job of hiding her voluptuous body. "Tortured and shotgunned in the face, like Mustafa Hasani."

Ritter exhaled loudly. Careful what you wish for, he thought.

"Where?" Ebeling said.

"Alte Rabenstrasse," Meike said, giving him a brief look. "This time it's scared tourists instead of scared commuters."

Ritter remembered the picturesque little jetty on the Alster River. At the peak of summer, he and Jenny had watched a beautiful sunset near the stop for traditional, flat-bottomed barges. The tour boats were painted red and white, with wooden decks and benches inside.

"Who was killed?" Ebeling said.

"That's where it gets interesting," Meike said, turning her pigtails back to Ritter. "His ID card says he's Michael Kopperschmidt, twenty-two years old, from Schnelsen. POLAS says he's a prospect of the Harbor City Chapter of the Hells Angels. Street name Mikey. His rap sheet includes arrests for aggravated assault, extortion, and distribution of controlled substances. No convictions."

"No convictions?" Ritter said.

"No witnesses," Meike says. "Every time Mikey Kopperschmidt came up on charges, the witnesses withdrew their testimony. It's not hard to figure out why."

Ritter smiled slightly. "Where's Harbor City?" he said. The name sounded American, like Mikey.

"That's what the Hamburg Chapter calls itself since it was outlawed," Meike said.

"They were forbidden from wearing their colors," Ebeling corrected her. "You know, those awful black leather vests with Gothic letters on the back," he added for Ritter.

"They know how to get around that," Meike said. "These days, they wear T-shirts with '81' on them. As in 'HA'. Kind of like the '88' T-shirts neo-Nazis wear for you-know-who. Anyhow, they're not on real friendly terms with the Hasani clan."

"What does that have to do with this killing?" Ebeling said.

"A shotgun blast to the face?" Meike said. "Two days in a row? Really?"

Ritter agreed. "I don't believe in coincidences," he said. At least Meike thought like a real cop. She followed leads, not orders.

"It looks like retaliation for Mustafa Hasani's killing," Meike said.

"Sulejman Hasani is serving a life sentence in Santa Fu," Ebeling reminded her. "And his top lieutenants are in U-Haft on suspicion of having killed Mustafa Hasani."

"The top brass doesn't normally do its own dirty work," Ritter said to Meike. "Usually, they delegate it to subordinates. You know, plausible deniability." He enjoyed the momentary flush on Ebeling's thin face.

Meike gave Ritter a knowing smile, her freckles beaming.

He knew she enjoyed Ebeling's discomfort, however fleeting.

"You'd better get down there, Herr Kriminalhauptkommissar,"

Ebeling said. "And take Motz Beck with you."

"What about me?" Meike said.

"You can put your recent computer training to work," Ebeling said, putting his hands on the inkblot and standing up. "Track the movements of this, um—"

"Mikey Kopperschmidt," Meike said.

"Yes," Ebeling said. "Find out where he's been lately."

Ritter actually agreed with the command.

"And do the same for Mustafa Hasani," Ebeling said.

"Already did," Meike said. "Mustafa visited his uncle like clockwork every Tuesday morning."

Ebeling looked up in surprise. "They allow weekly visits in Santa Fu?"

"They do if you pay off the guards," Meike said.

Ritter felt his own eyebrows shoot up.

"That sounds like wild speculation," Ebeling said and busied himself with the inkblot again.

"We'll be sure to get airtight evidence that will stand up in court," Ritter said, heading for the door. Meike let out a quiet giggle that made him wonder if she'd eavesdropped before knocking. "Shall we?" he said.

"You bet," Meike said and led the way back to their shared office at the working end of the hall.

THIRTEEN

Raven Street

"Mikey Kopperschmidt?" Motz said, whipping the wheel of the Charger through a stale yellow. "You know who that is, don't you?"

"A Hells Angels prospect," Ritter said.

"Not just that." Motz rubbed the scar in his scalp. "He's the half-brother of Lutz Kopperschmidt, the president of the Hamburg Chapter."

Motz knew Lutz all too well. The scar came from Lutz's motorcycle chain when both were sixteen. The Hells Angels had just "offered" Motz's father protection for his bar, Hansa Stuben, in St. Pauli. When Motz mouthed off about a shakedown, Lutz whipped off his stainless-steel O-ring belt and whacked him over the head, sending him to Hafenkrankenhaus for twenty-seven stitches and two weeks of antibiotics. After that, Willi Kaiser was "generous" enough to become a kind of godfather to Motz and a silent partner in his father's bar.

"Oh," Ritter said. "Meike didn't tell me that."

"What did she tell you?" Motz said, accelerating into the wide curve that took them around what a few weeks before had been the lush greenness of Stadtpark. Now the old oak trees flying by were turning colors against the morning sun. Like always, the red-brick planetarium in the middle stayed in place, like a lighthouse for lost detectives.

"She thinks Mikey Kopperschmidt is revenge for the hit on Mustafa Hasani," Ritter said. "That would make this a war between the Albanians and the Hells Angels."

"Or it's Sulejman Hasani covering his tracks," Motz said. "I wouldn't put it past him to be behind both murders. That's how he thinks. If in doubt, kill."

"That's conjecture," Ritter said. "We don't have any evidence that Hasani had his nephew killed."

"We have the surveillance tapes from Restaurant Engel," Motz said.

Ritter shook his head. "That was a beatdown, not murder. The Hells Angels could have been behind the shotgun."

"No," Motz said. "They would have taken out all four Hasanis at Restaurant Engel, not just Mustafa." He smiled coldly. "I know I would have."

"Try to keep it professional," Ritter said.

"Whatever you say, boss," Motz said, steering the pimpmobile onto Harvestehuder Weg.

Alsterpark on the left was full of golden leaves that some kids had formed into a small hill. One after the other, they were jumping on top, like Motz did when he was their age. Across the street was an overly modern music conservatory. The sign out front said: "Hochschule für Musik und Theater." The dark, curved concrete building looked like a gigantic whale preparing to swallow the kids in the leaves.

As the Charger approached Alte Rabenstrasse, Motz leaned on the horn. The early morning joggers, cyclists, and tourists clustered around the mouth of the jetty backed away reluctantly. The Charger nosed its way onto the sandy sidewalk and up to the crime scene tape.

Motz locked up the car because of the crowd. Wherever you found tourists, you found thieves.

Ritter was already on the jetty, hunched with the coroner behind a white tarp under the tour-boat schedule.

"*Moin*, Rudi," Motz said as he clomped up. "How's it hanging?"

"*Moin*, Motz," Rudi said. His cigar let out a puff of exertion as he struggled to his feet. "These bones aren't what they used to be." He was referring to his own less-than-limber body.

Behind him was the bloody corpse of another young man without a face. Unlike Mustafa Hasani, this one wasn't wearing a sharkskin suit, just a beat-to-shit black leather jacket, black T-shirt, black jeans, and engineering boots with scuff marks on the inner right ankle. Like Motz.

"Greetings from Teufelsbrück," Rudi said.

Motz nodded and tried to mentally compare the blood splatters on the jetty to those in the trunk of Mustafa Hasani's Lexus. He didn't get far. It was all just a big sloppy mess that was beginning to stink in the early morning sun. Under the crusting blood, he made out white Gothic script.

Harbor City

81

Hamburg

"So, Meike was right about the '81' T-shirts," Ritter said, standing back up.

Motz snorted. Why didn't people just call things what they were, he thought. These days, bikers were forced to use coded messages like spies. What was next, invisible ink? How did hiding the bad guys help the good guys?

Ritter turned to the coroner. "What are we looking at?" he said.

"Kneecaps pulverized by shotgun blasts," Rudi said, flicking life into the coals of his stubby cigar. Flakes of ash landed on white tarp. "The shotgun blast to the face was most likely the cause of death, although I can't rule out shock from the kneecappings."

"Another shotgun?" Ritter said.

"Or the same shotgun," Rudi said, the coal in his wide mouth glowing contentedly. "We can't do ballistics on shotgun shells. But every cop knows that."

Motz watched a barge steer clear of the jetty. No pickups at Alte Rabenstrasse this morning. Tourists were glued to the wide windows, holding up cameras and phones.

"ID?" Ritter said.

Motz turned back to him. "We already know—"

"Michael Kopperschmidt," Rudi said.

"How do we know?" Ritter said.

Motz snorted again.

Rudi held up a bagged ID card.

"When will you have a positive ID?" Ritter said.

"We already do," Rudi said. "The fingerprints match those in his police record."

Ritter nodded approval. "Time of death?"

"Based on body temperature, I'd say five o'clock," Rudi said. "Just before dawn."

"Like Mustafa Hasani," Motz said. "That means Hasani gave the order."

"We already talked about that," Ritter said.

"If it walks like a psychopath and talks like a psychopath," Motz said.

Ritter gave him a look.

"Well, I'll leave you gentlemen to your customer," Rudi said. With a loud wheeze, he reached down and grabbed his tool kit. He patted Motz's shoulder in passing.

. . .

While Ritter examined the body some more, Motz walked to the end of the jetty and called Meike, who picked up on the first ring. "I need you to check somebody's movements," he said.

"Already did," Meike said. "Guess where Mikey Kopperschmidt was twenty-four hours ago?"

"Where?"

"You're supposed to guess," she said coyly.

"Meike," Motz said. The talented young detective was proactive to a fault, but she liked to dramatize her results, drawing out conversations as long as possible.

"With Willi Kaiser," Meike said.

Oh shit, Motz thought. He hoped Willi wasn't mixed up in this. Then again, a visit from Mikey Kopperschmidt wasn't all *that* strange. Willi liked to hand the heavy work to "the boys," as he called them. The Hells Angels' obsession with respect made them excellent enforcers.

"What makes you so sure Mikey Kopperschmidt was with Willi Kaiser?" Motz said. "GPS gives you locations, not people." He looked back at Ritter, who was staring at him.

"Because he visited Mr. Wu's," Meike said knowingly.

"Oh." That was where Motz had made his big payoff to Willi six months earlier. He wondered how much Meike remembered about that. Probably everything. She was, after all, the one who had erased the recording from his phone before Internal Affairs got ahold of it. "When exactly?" he said.

"Mikey Kopperschmidt arrived at seven-fifty-three," Meike said. "And left at eight oh four."

"Thanks, Meike," Motz said and hung up.

When he turned around, Ritter was standing right in front of him.

"You get all that?" Motz said.

"Enough."

"Been too long since I last saw Willi," Motz said and clomped back to the Charger. That was the problem with partners, he thought, unlocking the driver's door. They heard everything you said—and everything you didn't.

FOURTEEN

Eye for an Eye

The Charger's fat tires meandered across cobblestones the size of half-buried skulls until the old red-brick restaurant came into view. The loose suspension made the chassis sway.

Motz killed the engine, yanked the emergency brake, and squeaked open the wide door. "This is it."

The passenger door slammed. Ritter was already marching toward the back door where Willi Kaiser's bodyguards were waiting. Motz hoped they weren't dumb enough to frisk him.

As Ritter badged the guards, his gun hand at the ready, Motz brushed by them and pulled open the screen door and led the way, clomping through the noisy kitchen, which was filled with the usual steamy clouds of exotic spices.

The owner, Mr. Wu, wasn't anywhere to be seen. Probably in his office, Motz thought, locking up the passports of his illegal workforce until they had paid him for their passage—with interest. Or he was watching Willi Kaiser through the black silk screen with the ancient orgy painted in gold behind his table.

Motz held back the red beads in the doorway for Ritter, who entered the dining room without comment. Willi's table took up half of the platform in the far corner. The old gangster was passing judgement on some terrified debtor who stood with bowed head, hands clasped in subservience. Willi motioned the poor soul away with fingernails that glistened in the reddish light. He must've moved up to high gloss, Motz thought.

A bodyguard grabbed the debtor by the back of the neck and walked him out a side door.

Willi made a show of dipping his fingertips into black tea and then wiping them methodically with a white linen napkin that a Chinese slave in a white dinner jacket held out for him. That meant Willi had already spotted them.

Ritter strode up to the table. "Polizei Hamburg," he said. "We're here about Mustafa Hasani."

Motz followed him reluctantly.

Willi wiped his mouth slowly with the napkin and then dropped it into the slave's waiting hands. Motz was pretty sure the slave didn't understand German, but he did seem fluent in raw animal power, bowing at the waist and disappearing like a shadow.

Only then did Willi raise his oversized black glasses to Ritter. "What can I do for you, Herr Kommissar?" he said.

"Where were you two nights ago at two thirty in the morning?" Ritter said.

Willi's big eyes weren't smiling as they drifted over to Motz. "What's this about?"

"Answer the question," Ritter said.

"We were getting our early morning Thai massage at Exotic Dream, just around the corner." Willi pointed a beefy hand at the two bodyguards who stood at the foot of the table. "You should try it sometime. It's a very relaxing way to end the day—or begin it."

The two bodyguards grinned at their boss's little joke.

"All of you?" Ritter said.

"I don't go anywhere without my associates," Willi said, giving Ritter his great-white-shark smile.

The bodyguards nodded in somber agreement with their boss's airtight alibi. They were all at Exotic Dream at the time in question.

"Did you order the execution of Mustafa Hasani?" Ritter said.

Motz watched Willi closely. He wasn't looking for signs of a second lie. He was waiting for his own cue.

"Who?" Willi's oily drawl had an ugly undertone.

Motz knew it was only a matter of minutes, if not seconds, before Willi used their "special relationship" to get around Ritter. A relationship based on blackmail.

Willi'd had the goods on Motz ever since he paid off a gambling debt to protect the lives of the widow and son of his murdered partner. Afterwards, Motz had sweated it out, expecting an anonymous call "requesting" something small, like a license plate check, anything that would implicate him. The call never came, but it was coming. Probably now, in front of Ritter. Motz ground his teeth.

"Mustafa Hasani," Ritter said. "You know, the kid without a face on Teufelsbrück." He turned to Motz. "Or the kid without a face on Alte Rabenstrasse. It's kind of hard to keep track."

Willi gave Motz a concerned look. "What's wrong with your partner? He doesn't seem right in the head."

"Answer the question, Willi," Motz said. "Did you put out a hit on Hasani's nephew?" The only way to deal with a blackmailer was frontal assault, he thought. If that didn't work, you put a gun to his head. If that didn't work, you pulled the trigger. This was something he should have done a long time ago. Now circumstances were forcing his hand.

"You know me better than that," Willi said.

There were three ways to read the seemingly innocuous non-answer. One: Willi knew things about Motz that would interest Internal Affairs. Two: Willi thought Motz would protect him to save his own skin. Three: Willi wasn't stupid enough to piss on Hasani's leg.

Motz decided to go with Door Number Three. "That's the problem," he said. "We know you too well. Even if we can't prove it, we know you fire-bombed your former accountant's office the night Hasani was arrested. You know, the accountant who worked for Hasani at your expense."

"Is this some kind of joke?" Willi said, his big eyes blazing.

"I look like I'm joking?" Motz said, returning Willi's hot stare with a cold one. Fuck blackmail. He paused long enough for Willi to snort at the white tablecloth. "The kind of guy who attacks Hasani when he's arrested is the kind of guy who attacks Hasani when he's convicted. See the problem, Willi?"

"You should talk," Willi shot back. "You and your funny money."

Motz moved to the table fast enough to make Willi's bodyguards look to him for orders. "You got something you want to say, Willi?" he said. "Or you just want to play games?"

Willi slammed the table with his meaty fist. The chopsticks in front of him jumped. "What the hell is this!" he yelled. A tea stain grew in front of him. The Chinese slave didn't return to clean it up.

Willi's show of anger told Motz he was just trying to save face. If Willi was going to drop the dime on him, he would have done it calmly with a sweet smile on his face.

"You tell me," Motz said. "We're investigating two torture murders. One of theirs, one of yours. We already talked to—"

"One of mine?" Willi said, his eyes wide enough to indicate surprise. Or maybe it was just the glasses.

"Mikey Kopperschmidt," Motz said.

"Who the hell is that?" Willi said.

"Hells Angels prospect," Motz said. "You know, the kid who

visited you here yesterday morning." He felt Ritter's eyes on him.

Willi shook his head. His face was getting red with the exertion of keeping his big jaw clamped shut.

"First a Hasani, then an Angel," Motz said. "Looks like tit for tat."

"I thought you were smarter than that, Motz," Willi said.

"So you didn't order the killing of Mustafa Hasani?" Ritter said, holding up his hand to Motz. My turn.

Motz shrugged. Let Ritter beat a dead horse. Willi didn't appear to be involved.

"No, I didn't order the killing of Mustafa Hasani," Willi said. He looked at Motz. "Or anyone else."

"Not even Mikey Kopperschmidt?" Ritter said.

Motz returned Willi's look. They both knew Ritter was way off on that one.

"No," Willi said. "Like I just told you, nobody else."

"We *will* verify your alibi," Ritter said.

"You want some friendly advice?" Willi said to Motz. His tone was fatherly now.

Motz squinted at him. Now what?

"Watch your back," Willi said. "Hasani's a snake. He's most dangerous when he's cornered. And you're the guy who backed him into a corner—for life."

Motz nodded. The old gangster was right about that. Nobody, not even homicide detectives and their families, would be one hundred percent safe until the Albanian boss was under the ground, where he belonged.

PETER SARDA

FIFTEEN

The Expert

"So we've got nothing," Ritter said, hitting the elevator button in the underground parking garage.

"I wouldn't say that," Motz said. "We've got the Hasanis."

The two of them had gone through the logical possibilities on the drive back to the Polizeipräsidium. Although Motz continued to believe that the Hasanis themselves had killed Mustafa, he had no real evidence, just painful personal experience with the clan's brutal business practices. Obviously, the three thugs they'd interrogated harshly at Casino Esplanade couldn't have killed Mikey Kopperschmidt because they were in U-Haft at the time of his death.

The other possibility, according to Ritter, was Willi Kaiser, but Motz didn't buy it. Willi's warning underlined the point. He was as wary of Hasani as anybody else.

Which led back to Motz's original theory. After killing his nephew for some infraction of "honor," Hasani killed a Hells Angel just to throw the cops off the trail and let Willi Kaiser know he was as lethal as ever.

Ritter didn't buy the double murder theory, but he didn't know Hasani the way Motz did. For Hasani, killing was a primary means of communication. It was always a statement.

The doors clanged open. The two detectives stepped into the large elevator. Its walls were carpeted, as though to muffle hush-hush conversations about confidential investigations. Motz hit 6. The doors shut with a dull bang, and they were jerked upward.

"We can only hold the Hasanis for two more days," Ritter said. "Assuming the state prosecutor plays ball."

"We've got them on film kicking the shit out of Mustafa," Motz said. "And they assaulted two detectives."

The elevator jerked to a stop. The doors opened.

"That's pretty thin," Ritter said, stepping into the cool hallway. "You know how the state prosecutor ticks."

"Yeah," Motz said. "She always protects the guilty from the innocent."

"The Hasanis are the ones with the cuts and bruises," Ritter reminded him.

Motz smiled at the memory of the three Albanian gangsters plastic-cuffed on the ground. "Sometimes there *is* justice," he said. With that happy thought, he followed Ritter into their office.

"Ebeling called another meeting," Meike said from her desk.

"Good afternoon to you too," Motz said.

"No, it's not," she said. "The state prosecutor just released the Hasanis from U-Haft."

"What!" Motz and Ritter said at the same time.

"Insufficient evidence," Meike said. "Ebeling claims he knew nothing about their 'mistreatment,' as he called it."

"You're shitting me," Motz said, trading looks with Ritter. "We're talking about the goddamn Hasanis." But he knew that Ebeling—let alone the state prosecutor—was more than capable of throwing them to the rat squad without notice. Both seemed to take perverse pleasure in hindering justice and frustrating detectives.

There was a knock at the doorframe. Ebeling. The bastard was smiling. At his shoulder was a guy in a brown suit. Alone. That was strange. Normally, the rat squad travelled in pairs.

"I'd like to introduce you to someone," Ebeling said. He stood aside and guided his guest into the room. "This is Kriminalhauptkommissar Wolf."

Motz took a closer look. The suit was rumpled corduroy. Underneath was some kind of raggedy-ass T-shirt that wasn't even tucked in, the kind rich-at-thirty startup types wore. KHK Wolf looked a fit fifty, except for the black rings under slightly amused brown eyes that didn't flinch. His short, grizzled hair somehow matched his hook nose, olive-colored skin, laconic posture, and well-oiled work boots, which looked like they'd been resoled at least once. Motz exhaled. This definitely wasn't the rat squad.

"KHK Wolf is an expert on drug gangs in Hamburg," Ebeling continued. "He's on loan to us from the Narcotics Division."

Motz found that hard to believe. Wolf didn't look like a drug guy either. More like a university professor with a complicated double life and a penchant for violence. Motz couldn't quite find a category for him. Which may have been the point. Somebody that unique could do well in rough neighborhoods like St. Pauli where authenticity was everything and social status nothing.

Ebeling's expert stepped forward in a half swagger and gave a firm handshake to each of the detectives with a tilted head and a twinkle in his eye. "Wolf," he said.

"Ritter."

"Motz."

"Voss."

Wolf seemed amused by Meike's rain boots. She was wearing lime green today.

Motz caught a sharp whiff of nicotine off the old brown suit. Like Hansa Stuben when his old man opened up back in the day.

"KHK Wolf will be helping us with our two drug-related homicide investigations," Ebeling said. "Think of him as a kind of consultant."

"*Two* drug-related homicides?" Ritter said. "Only one involves drugs, as far as we know."

"Exactly," Ebeling said. "As far as you know. KHK Wolf has been kind enough to fill me in on the background of the two victims. Both are directly linked to the sale of dangerous narcotics to young people." He looked at Wolf, who nodded back, this time without a smile. His eyes were ice cold.

"We found drugs on Mustafa Hasani—" Ritter said.

"Rainbow," Wolf said.

"—but not on Mikey Kopperschmidt."

"We know that Mikey Kopperschmidt was selling Rainbow to students at the University of Hamburg," Wolf said. "Through intermediaries who are themselves students."

His hoarse drawl reminded Motz of bikers who got friendly before they whacked you over the head with a motorcycle chain. But his words were precisely calibrated. Motz bet he was great on the witness stand. His sentences would check off all the boxes in the indictment.

"They target kids at discos and private parties in better neighborhoods like Eppendorf and Pöseldorf," Wolf continued.

Ebeling nodded approvingly at the word "better."

Motz snorted at the nodding. Ebeling and his upper-class bullshit. City Hall was like an old boys' club to him.

"Yeah, I know," Wolf said. "It seems like City Hall only cares about the children of wealthy donors, not the sons and daughters of dock workers, bus drivers, and shoemakers."

Ebeling stopped nodding.

Shoemakers. Motz grinned. That explained the boots. Wolf might work out, after all.

"Do you have any tangible evidence that Mikey Kopperschmidt was distributing Rainbow?" Ritter said.

"That's part of an ongoing undercover operation," Wolf said. "I can't get into the details. Need to know and all that."

Uh-oh, Motz thought. Wolf was talking like Ebeling now. Bottom-dwelling homicide detectives didn't need to know what their masters were doing.

"Why didn't anybody tell us?" Ritter demanded.

"I just did," Wolf said, amusement back in his eyes.

"Let me get this straight," Ritter said. "You know both murders are related to Rainbow, but you can't go into the details when talking to the very detectives assigned to investigate the murders. Am I getting this right?"

"Herr Ritter!" Ebeling objected.

"Yes," Wolf said to Ritter. "That is exactly right. My hands are bound by my own superiors. You know how that goes."

Ebeling looked like he had bitten into something bitter.

Motz grinned again. He had the strange urge to bum a cigarette off Wolf. He hadn't thought about a smoke since his first daughter was born.

"So, how can you help us?" Ritter said.

"By guiding the investigation," Ebeling said.

"What!" Ritter said. "This is the Homicide Division, not Narcotics."

"I said guiding, not leading, Herr Ritter."

"Good," Ritter said.

"I'm glad you agree," Ebeling said. "I'm asking Motz Beck to take over the investigation. For the time being"

"What!" Motz said.

Ritter shook his head in disgust.

Wolf gave a shrug that said: Whatcha gonna do?

"Beck, I want you and Voss to work with KHK Wolf," Ebeling said.

"What about Ritter?" Motz said. "He's our team leader." He could feel Meike nodding agreement.

"That was a direct order, Herr Oberkommissar."

Motz snorted. "Okey dokey."

Meike suppressed a giggle.

"Herr Ritter," Ebeling said. "I want to see you in my office. We need to talk about Copenhagen."

Ritter stared at Ebeling long enough for Motz to wonder if he was going to hit the arrogant prick.

"One more thing," Ebeling said, breaking in on his thoughts. "I want to be informed of every move you make in the field. Understood?"

Motz nodded but kept his eyes on Ritter, who followed Ebeling out the door without a word.

There was a light *tap-tap-tap* across the room. At a half-open window, Wolf was tapping down the tobacco of a filterless cigarette on his thumbnail.

"There's no smoking in the building," Meike said. "Everybody just goes outside."

"You mean the garage," Wolf said, sticking the cigarette behind his ear. "Care to join me?"

"Twist my arm," Meike said, grabbing her coat.

Over the years, Motz had noticed that Meike never bought her own cigarettes, choosing instead to bum them off male coworkers. He sometimes wondered if that was her real source of information. Even with her super-duper computer skills, she couldn't bug the whole Präsidium.

Wolf turned to Motz. "Kriminaloberkommissar?"

"Motz."

"Motz," Wolf said.

"Yeah, why not," Motz said. "You meet the most interesting people outside." He couldn't believe he said it. Of course, he hadn't actually committed to smoking, just hanging out in the garage. What was wrong with that?

Wolf smiled broadly. "After you."

Already, Motz knew Wolf had taken charge. That was just as well with him. Like Ritter said, they weren't getting anywhere on their own. And Wolf had a lot of inside information.

PETER SARDA

SIXTEEN

Hoochie Coochie Man

While Ebeling tormented Ritter on the sixth floor, KHK Wolf gave Motz and Meike the lowdown on his own investigation in the underground garage. The pristine brass upstairs might think they were running things, but the greasy mechanics in the engine room below decks were the ones who did the real work, steering the ship through treacherous waters.

From what Motz could tell, Wolf was the perfect mechanic. While chain smoking, he explained the complex rivalries between the Albanian, Lebanese, Turkish, Kurdish, Russian, Serbian, and German gangs, each of which controlled different illegal activities in different parts of town.

"What they all have in common is greed," Wolf said. "Have you ever met a gangster who wouldn't kill over a ridiculously small amount of money?" His Camel glowed brightly between his teeth. He was that kind of smoker. All teeth, no lips.

Motz had thought the same thing himself. Over the years, he'd been repeatedly surprised by the peevishness of Hasani, who talked like a pale bookkeeper but acted like a wild animal.

Wolf continued, a professor satisfied with alert students. The problem, of course, was the endless competition for the *same* illegal activities in the *same* parts of town. He picked an example familiar to Motz and Meike.

"Sulejman Hasani wanted to take over Willi Kaiser's whorehouse imperium," he said. "And Kaiser wanted to take over Hasani's gambling operation. Kaiser couldn't allow some Albanian upstart to take away his throne in St. Pauli, and Hasani couldn't afford for Kaiser to take over his casino. Hasani needed the casino to launder the massive profits he made from importing Afghan Gold so he could buy off the Hamburg Senate. And the Hamburg Senate needed the money to buy up and gentrify Kaiser's turf in St. Pauli. War was inevitable."

"Goddamn real estate," Motz said.

"Silicon Alley," Meike said, referring to the name the political sponsors had given the business park they planned to build.

Wolf beamed at them. "I can see you've done your homework."

Don't bullshit a bullshitter, Motz thought. Wolf was telling them about their own case six months earlier. Motz felt Meike's look as Wolf went into a coughing fit. Apparently Motz had said it out loud.

Wolf waved away the cough. "You're right," he said, gasping. "I just wanted to make sure we were on the same page."

"No," Motz said. "You wanted to show us you know everything we know."

Wolf coughed some more.

Still, Motz was impressed. Wolf was openly saying that he didn't trust Ebeling's bosses in City Hall. It was quite a statement coming from somebody just brought in by Ebeling.

"What's your real agenda?" Meike said, suspicion in her eyes and voice.

"Well," Wolf said carefully. He seemed to be testing his scratchy throat for a cough. "I need to know where you stand."

"What?" Meike said. "Who the hell are you to—"

Motz held up a hand. "Hold up, Meike."

"But—"

"Let the man speak," Motz said. Wolf had gone out on a limb. He needed to see if he could trust *them* before getting to what he really wanted to say.

Wolf cleared his throat loudly, like a preemptive attack on a new cough. "We can't stop a drug war without taking off the gloves."

"Who are you talking about?" Motz said. He hoped Wolf didn't mean Willi Kaiser.

"The Hasanis and the Hells Angels," Wolf said. "They're the ones selling Rainbow. Who did you think?"

"They're fighting over Rainbow?" Motz said, sidestepping the question. At least Willi Kaiser was off Wolf's radar.

"Of course," Wolf said. "But look at the past two days. They're killing each other off."

"That's a working theory," Motz said.

"No, it's reality," Wolf countered. "And we all know it." He patted his pockets for more cigarettes but just came up with an empty pack. He crunched it up and threw it onto the polished concrete, next to half a dozen ground-out butts. "Can we take this someplace else?" he said. "I gotta restock."

Motz nodded. "I know just the place." He looked at Meike. "You up to Hansa Stuben?"

"I guess so," Meike said, a funny look in her eye. "I could use a double vodka." It was pretty obvious she still didn't trust Wolf.

"Sounds like a plan," Wolf said.

The three of them walked up the ramp to the third post, where Motz's Charger was waiting.

"Nice wheels," Wolf said. "But I've got my own." He pointed to a perfectly restored Mercedes with a glistening brown finish.

Motz squinted at the trademark grill facing out. "Sixty-eight?"

"That's right," Wolf said. "It's kind of a family heirloom."

"I've got my own car," Meike said, chirping her fire-engine red Fiat 500. The front lights blinked. She got in without another word and slammed the door.

Wolf's grin showed nicotine-stained teeth. "This could be the beginning of a beautiful friendship," he said.

Not so fast, Motz thought as he keyed the door to the Charger. The jury was still out on Wolf.

■ ■ ■

"That really you?" Meike was leaning her bulky sweater halfway over the bar, gesturing at the small framed black-and-white photo on the wall next to the old mechanical cash register. In the center was an iconic photo of Baby Motz in a cloth-lined wicker basket, the soles of his white-socked feet facing the camera. "It looks like he's keeping pace with the beat."

"Yup," Motz said, wiping beer foam from his upper lip. The moment they'd walked into the bar, he'd dumped a handful of coins into the old Wurlitzer jukebox. Thank God some things didn't change. It was still loaded with the same classic blues he grew up with. Now it was blasting "Boom Boom" by John Lee Hooker.

"You were so cute!" Meike said.

Wolf laughed into his beer and sucked the life out his Camel, which had a silent death in the overflowing Jägermeister ashtray.

Despite the citywide ban on smoking, Hansa Stuben was still a smokers' bar, like in the bad old days. Willi Kaiser got around the ban by registering it as a "smoking club." He then got a new liquor license to serve "club members and guests."

Motz raised an eyebrow at Meike. "You mean I ain't cute no more?"

While Wolf fired up another death stick, Meike gave Motz an up-and-down look that made him suck in his gut. "More manly," she concluded.

Motz nodded and exhaled.

"I'll drink to that," Wolf said and whirled his finger in the air.

The bartender nodded back and started preparing another round. First he put two fresh beer mugs under the tap. Then he walked over with the half-empty bottle of Stolichnaya.

Motz didn't recognize him. The muscle pack with the shaved skull must be one of Willi Kaiser's guys. Under his olive-green T-shirt, his left arm was covered with tattoos down to the wrist. His right arm was free of any marks—if you didn't count the bulging veins. Motz figured him for a steroid freak.

Meike held her hand over her tumbler. "No more for me. It's a work night." She looked at Motz. "For me at least."

"Too late," Wolf said and downed his shot. "Might as well keep the bottle here," he added to the bartender.

Motz laughed but left his shot glass alone. For the past hour, Wolf had been chasing Stolichnaya with Hacker-Pschorr Pilsner like there was no tomorrow.

Meike squeezed into her green leather jacket, pushed her pigtails over the collar, and swiveled off her stool. "See you tomorrow," she said to Motz.

Wolf raised his next shot to her and downed it.

Meike brushed Motz with a hard sleeve that left a pleasant mix of leather aroma and light perfume in its wake. "Say hi to Sabine," she said.

Motz sighed. Meike didn't mention his wife for no reason. She was probably beginning to worry. "Gotta call the wife," he said to Wolf, watching Meike get hit on at the front door by a dock worker in blue coveralls. Motz slid off his stool and headed toward the john, his phone out.

Wolf nodded and drained his Hacker-Pschorr mug, leaving foam behind the *Himmel der Bayern* banner.

Motz smiled to himself. Out-of-towners always asked his

father why they stocked Bavarian beer. St. Pauli was as far from Lederhosen as you could get. The answer was simple. The beer really did taste like heaven. Of course, Motz had long since graduated to Flensburger Pilsener. The bitter Northern German beer better matched his taste and temperament. On the job at least. He hit "Honeybee" on his phone.

"Hey, stranger!" a smoky voice said after two rings.

"Hey," Motz said, one eye on Wolf. The guy was pouring himself another shot. "Had a late meeting."

Sabine laughed. "I can hear that."

Muddy Waters was now belting out "Hoochie Coochie Man" on the jukebox.

"Offsite meeting," Motz said. "I'm on my way home soon."

"You want me to pick you up?" Sabine said. "The girls are already in bed."

"I'll call a cab," Motz said. "Just gotta finish up here."

Sabine laughed again. "Don't finish up too much! You're not thirty anymore."

"Don't I know it," Motz said. "Love you."

"Love you more," she said.

"Love you most." Motz put away his phone but didn't walk back to the bar.

Wolf had just snorted something off the back of his hand. Like when Motz drove past his Mercedes in the garage at the Präsidium. Motz doubted it was snuff.

It was an open secret that Narcotics guys sometimes dipped into their favorite "products." It looked like Wolf was a coke head. That would explain his inability to get drunk on half a dozen U-boats downed in rapid succession.

Motz meandered back to the bar and slipped back onto the well-worn leather again. "Miss me?" he said.

"Thought you fell in," Wolf said. His tone said something else.

"Uh-huh," Motz said. Apparently, Wolf knew he was being watched. Motz had to be careful with that. Despite his erratic behavior, the seasoned detective was as sharp as the straight edge Motz tested when he was nine. The thing nearly took his fingertip off.

"I was just thinking about clan structures," Wolf said. No transition. For once, he wasn't smoking or drinking.

Motz was wide awake now. Even the jukebox had gone silent.

"Clans are living, breathing things," Wolf continued. "The only way to destroy them is to pull them out by the roots."

Wolf was beginning to sound like Motz when he was on a rampage. Except, as Sabine always said, Motz's anger peaked quickly. He just needed to get it out, to be heard.

Wolf, on the other hand, was slow-burning, always moving in one direction, toward something big and irreversible. Even his anger was methodical. He probably had his stages of rage all charted out.

"Ever tell you about my chart?" Wolf said.

"Uh, no," Motz said. Maybe Wolf was snorting some kind of brain steroid. The guy seemed to read thoughts. Probably had a hundred percent clearance rate. Motz would have to ask Meike about that in the morning. Knowing her, she had already started a file on Wolf.

"Got it on my wall," Wolf said, nodding at something Motz couldn't see. "The whole Rainbow chain of command, from the lowliest Hells Angels prospect to the president of the Harbor City Chapter. Same for the Albanians."

"That I'd like to see," Motz said. Especially the Hasani side of the chart, he thought. He remembered that garage in *A Beautiful Mind* at the Savoy Cinema. Thousands of flashcards connected by thousands of strings. It was madness on the big screen.

At least Wolf was on their side. They were going to need all the help they could get on this one. Unless Motz's gut was mistaken, the killing had only just begun.

PETER SARDA

SEVENTEEN

Body Count

The wide tires of the Charger slipped over hidden train tracks in the misty dawn. Through the hand-streaked windshield, Motz could make out cranes and rows of containers stacked high enough to block the weak sunlight on Steinwerder.

Behind the mist was the depot where they repaired old cargo containers—and tortured detectives. The scars on his wrists twitched uneasily.

He glanced at Ritter, who seemed lost in thought. Probably retracing his own steps six months earlier.

The Charger maneuvered the tight right–left–right–left that led to the rusty "Do Not Enter" sign. Motz laughed mirthlessly. How appropriate.

On that fateful night, he hadn't seen the warning, even with the full moon, because they'd put a smelly hood over his pounding skull. The gaping wound from the pistol butt required five stitches to the back of his buzzcut. It was his second visit to the emergency ward in almost thirty years. This wound healed better than the first, but it bothered him more.

He tried not to look at the red container at the top of the last row. He wondered if his blood was still splattered on the corrugated steel inside. Then he remembered. Container renovation was like witness relocation. First, steam-cleaning that required waterproof coveralls and hoods, then industrial paint sprayed through nozzles that made masks and goggles mandatory. After that, the containers were all but untraceable.

Up ahead were half a dozen patrol cars and Forensics vans clustered around three bodies. KHK Wolf was standing near the first body, facing the misty sun with closed eyes, dragging on a cigarette. Rudi was kneeling over the third body, examining something with a small flashlight.

Motz killed the engine, swung open his door, and stepped onto gritty wet concrete that crunched under his boots.

Ritter was already surveying the crime scene.

They were greeted by a uniform with steaming hands.

"Thanks," Motz said, gratefully taking the first paper cup. He hadn't wanted to wake his wife and daughters so early, even on a school day, so he left the house without his usual pick-me-up. The coffee from the uniform was black and harsh, like his mood.

"What've we got?" Ritter said, ignoring the cup offered to him.

"Three DOAs," the uniform said, pointing at the bodies.

Ritter nodded and headed toward the first body. Motz followed.

Wolf's cigarette sparked on gravel as he gave Motz a friendly heads-up. Ebeling's expert seemed to have made a hell of a recovery. If Motz had dumped that much Stoli down his gullet, he'd be in ICU with a pumped stomach and tubes up his nose.

"*Moin moin*," Motz said, getting a closer look at the bodies, which had been torn apart by what he guessed was yet more shotgun fire. Plastic numbers marked a small number of shell casings, which might indicate return fire. "Glad I didn't eat breakfast," he said.

"Good thing you saved your appetite," Wolf said. "We've got a lovely buffet for you this morning. First up on the menu is one Manhar Hasani."

"Sulejman Hasani's enforcer," Ritter said from his crouched position.

Motz bristled. The oversized body belonged to the thug he had pistol-whipped and hog-tied three days earlier. One of the three Hasanis the state prosecutor had released from U-Haft the night before. The enforcer had a glistening skull, thick beard, taped-up nose with cotton inside, stitches in one cheek, some kind of plaster mesh on the other, and two black eyes that were beginning to yellow. And a hole the size of a fist where his stomach should have been.

Wolf turned and pointed an unlit cigarette at a second suited animal. "That enrichment to humanity was Employee of the Month at Casino Esplanade," he said. "Used to be Besnik Hasani." His voice was muffled by his Zippo, which cracked open and torched the cigarette.

Ritter shot him an unfriendly look and walked over to the second body.

"Based on their last names, I'd guess they're related," Wolf continued. "Wouldn't you?"

"Can the commentary," Ritter said, but Wolf had already sauntered off.

Motz stepped around the first body and over to where Ritter was now crouched. The second body looked similar to the first, except it was even bigger. And half its skull was missing. It was the giant Ritter had knocked down at the casino. The second Hasani released from U-Haft. The state prosecutor was really racking up the body count this morning.

"And *thiiis* piece of work," Wolf said from a distance, "is James Hasani. What an exotic name, huh? James."

"That's enough," Ritter said.

Wolf shrugged.

Motz squinted at the third body. It was the third thug from

Casino Esplanade. The state prosecutor was now three for three. Not bad for an overly ambitious do-gooder.

"His real name was Jacob," Wolf said. "But everybody called him James." He was standing next to the coroner, who pocketed his flashlight and struggled to his feet.

"Probably nicknamed after James Belushi," Rudi said, looking at his latest "customer" with no expression on his face. "Bet you didn't know the Belushi family came from Albania."

"Who?" Motz said, walking up.

"*Saturday Night Live*," Rudi said. "Before your time."

Motz crouched down and examined another gaping chest wound. His eyes moved up to the face. This thug looked even unhappier than he had when Motz hit him upside the head with his P6.

"Cause of death?" Ritter said.

"All three were killed instantly by shotgun blasts," Rudi said, relighting his stubby cigar.

Motz was grateful for more tobacco in the air on a morning like this. Even outdoors, so much blood and guts got into your nose and stayed there for days.

"They got off a few rounds on the way down," Wolf said, pointing to the plastic numbers.

"Not enough to matter," the Forensics guy said.

"You think it was just reflex?" Ritter said.

"Yeah," the Forensics guy said. "All they had were small caliber handguns. They didn't stand a chance."

"Too bad for them," Wolf said.

■ ■ ■

While Ritter walked the perimeter of the crime scene, scanning the ground for something, Motz decided to regroup with Wolf, who was standing by himself.

Wolf pocketed his phone a bit too quickly and said, "Got a minute?"

Motz frowned. "What's up?"

"Got something to show you," Wolf said. "Won't take long."

"What is it?"

"My surprise," Wolf said, walking away.

Motz was about to call out when Wolf ducked behind a row of containers. Now what?

A few seconds later, a diesel engine started up. Exhaust made its way around the containers, followed by the grill of the Mercedes.

Ritter stopped his perimeter walk. "Where the hell is Wolf going?" he yelled.

"He wants to show me something," Motz yelled back.

Ritter shook his head.

"He says it won't take long," Motz added, but Ritter was back to his perimeter.

A genteel toot from Wolf's horn sent Motz back to his Charger. With a spray of gravel, he followed the Mercedes back through the maze of Steinwerder and Kleiner Grasbrook, back to the elevated safety of Lombardsbrücke.

Motz's hand was on the radio dial when the Mercedes signaled at Elbbrücken. He followed it through the dizzying offramp and onto Versmanstrasse. It looked like Wolf was heading for HafenCity.

A few minutes later, the Mercedes pulled into the "No Parking" zone outside the new HafenCity University complex. Motz did the same, putting a blue plastic "Polizei Hamburg – Official Business" sign on the dash before locking up. He knew traffic cops were especially diligent in upscale districts like this.

Wolf was already on the sidewalk. "Nice neighborhood," he said. "But too rich for my blood."

Motz squinted at him. "What's this all about?"

Wolf grinned back. "You'll see." With that, he walked away, along the banks of Baakenhafen, in the long shadow of concrete condos.

As Motz followed, he took in the burglar-friendly display of wealth surrounding him. Where he grew up, they had bars on the windows. Nothing to lose but everything to fear. He wondered how much the security guys in HafenCity made. Probably double the income of homicide detectives who barely made mortgage payments on modest houses in the suburbs.

EIGHTEEN

The Penthouse

Wolf sliced through the red-and-white coat of arms on the Polizei Hamburg seal with a pocketknife and turned over the armored cross-bolt like he owned the penthouse. The polished-brass plate next to the buzzer read: "M. Hasani."

Motz grinned. Punk gangsters like Mustafa Hasani were afraid of burglars too. He wondered when Wolf had signed out the Class 5 reversible keys from the property room. Had he planned to show Motz the condo? Or was he just a frequent visitor?

The door opened onto a panoramic view of the Hamburg skyline, from the postmodern Elbphilharmonie, to the landmark St. Michaelis Church, to the baroque City Hall, to the traditional red-brick Speicherstadt warehouse district, to the main train station, to the old Grossmarkt, to the new HafenCity University.

"Wow," Motz said. "I guess crime really does pay." He was a bit surprised at his own enthusiasm. Normally, he didn't think much of the dickheads in HafenCity. But the view, my God. Wait until he told Sabine. He stopped short. Better not. She would ask why he hadn't taken pictures.

"You haven't seen anything," Wolf said, trailing smoke to the wall of windows. "The punk has a sunken Carrara marble bathtub the size of a small swimming pool. It's even got gold-plated faucets. He imported the marble from Tuscany. You believe that shit?" Wolf sounded cheerful, but there was no admiration in his voice. He seemed to be tormenting himself with Mustafa Hasani's wealth.

Motz clomped over to the windows.

"Turn around," Wolf commanded, his voice echoing against cold marble.

Motz did as he was told—and almost fell over. The entire harbor stared back at him from the wall of windows on the other side. Veddel, Kleiner Grasbrook, Steinwerder, where they had just examined the shotgunned bodies, and, further down the Elbe River, Finkenwerder and the Airbus plant. "Man-oh-man-oh-man," he said. "This place really belonged to Mustafa Hasani?"

"None of this will do him any good where he is now," Wolf said. He took a long drag on his cigarette for emphasis.

"Burning in hell would be my guess," Motz said. Along with Hasani's ex-bodyguard, he thought. Six months earlier, the big shadow in the container had exhaled garlic as he pressed a .38 into Motz's bloody temple. Ritter dropped the animal with one to the head and two to the chest. Another closed casket.

The walls and furniture of the luxury apartment had black powder residue where Forensics had dusted for prints. Mostly Mustafa Hasani's numerous cousins and expensive escort girls, all of whom were registered in the POLAS database.

One surprise was a university student. Or not, Motz thought. Expensive trophy wives with little rat-dogs were getting a run for their money from all the cute girls in too-tight T-shirts and strategically torn cutoffs running around HafenCity these days.

"My tribe says hell is one big nothing," Wolf said. "You just float in dark, silent space for eternity." He ground his cigarette butt into hardwood, crossed the living room again, and opened a ridiculously wide sliding glass door onto a wide balcony that ran the entire length of the apartment.

"That works for me," Motz said. He could see the hardwood was the real thing, not the cheap-ass parquet flooring Sabine complained about when they first met. She said it caused over fifty percent of the conflicts between apartment house residents. The grainy slats under his feet looked like walnut. They matched the cabinets above the steel-topped surfaces in the kitchen.

Motz followed Wolf onto the balcony, where he was hit by a gust of wind. They were only six floors up, but the building was right on the harbor. "Jesus Christ," he said. "How could Mustafa afford all this? He was just Hasani's courier."

"Rainbow," Wolf said.

"Sales must've been good," Motz said.

"His girlfriend introduced him to university students," Wolf said. "She took him to inside parties and discos." His dark eyes narrowed. "Being a Hasani, Mustafa couldn't resist selling poison to his new high-life friends. His girlfriend ended up getting her stomach pumped at Hammonia Hospital. That was the end of their relationship. But, by that point, the little shit didn't need her anymore."

Something about the story bothered Motz. "How do you know all this?"

"Sunday School," Wolf said.

"Got it," Motz said. "Need to know."

Wolf pointed to something in the distance, barely visible from the left side of the balcony. "That's where I grew up," he said. "Barmbek. My old man was a shoemaker. My mom was a seamstress. Salt of the earth."

"A shoemaker, huh?" Motz said, impressed again by his own ability to read people. He pointed his thumb in the opposite direction, to St. Pauli. "That's where I grew up," he said. "But you already know that."

Wolf laughed. "Was that really you in the wicker basket? You don't look anything like Moses."

Motz smiled and fingered the scar in his scalp. "Yup. They kept me under the tap with all the kegs. To this day, I can't sleep without some kind of noise. My wife finally bought me one of those white noise machines for babies."

"I hear that," Wolf said. "My own basket was under my mom's sewing machine. Every time I hear one of those things, I want to close my eyes and go to sleep."

"No shit," Motz said happily. Wolf was alright. Just a hardworking cop who had seen too much. But underneath all that was a decent guy. Hell, Motz had been down that road himself.

A cloud passed overhead.

"Yeah, this used to be a great town," Wolf said.

"Before the Hasanis arrived," Motz agreed.

"Don't forget the Russian mafia."

"And the Lebanese clans," Motz said. Those fuckers were as scary as Hasani. Well, almost.

"And the Serbian mob," Wolf said. "With all that talk about Milošević and ethnic cleansing."

"And the Hells Angels," Motz said. If Willi wasn't careful, they would take over Kaiser Enterprises.

"And the African drug dealers. You know, the so-called asylum seekers in Schanzenpark."

"And St. Georg."

"And the Hauptbahnhof."

"And the jihadis," Motz said. Like that crazy Afghani who yelled "Allah akbar" as he went after uniforms with a machete.

Wolf didn't say anything. His eyes were bitter again.

"You okay?" Motz said.

Wolf shook his head. "They're winning, and we're losing."

Motz had to admit he was right. Maybe that was the point of this little visit. Maybe this had nothing to do with the killings. Maybe Wolf just wanted to get it off his chest. God knew, Motz felt like that too often.

"The state prosecutor always says we don't have enough evidence," Wolf said. "And the judges set wild animals loose on technicalities."

"Tell me about it," Motz said. How many times had that happened to him? He'd lost count. And Sabine wondered why he was cynical.

"We put up with it for too long," Wolf said. "We were too proper, too by the book."

Motz grunted agreement. He'd had this conversation with lots of cops, always in the privacy of a basement den or country cabin. The wind whistled menacingly. He felt the beginning of an earache.

"It's time somebody did something," Wolf said. "Somebody needs to clean up this cesspool."

Motz grunted again, but his experience disagreed. He *had* been doing something. If it wasn't for the state prosecutor and all her talk about "airtight evidence," he would have mopped the floor with half the bad guys in town by now.

"I say we round up the whole lot of them," Wolf said.

"Amen to that," Motz said, feeling nothing. This was just more big talk. It wouldn't change a thing. Still, it got you through the day. Sometimes, that was all that mattered.

"I say we go after all of them," Wolf continued. "First the Hasanis in their casinos, then the Russians in their titty bars."

"Then the Gray Wolves in their shisha bars," Motz said rotely.

"Then the Hells Angels in their meth labs."

"Then the senators on the take."

"Then the prosecutors who don't prosecute."

"Then the judges who don't judge."

"Yeah, this time, we'll go after the whole pack," Wolf said, using his hand to show the expanse of the city.

"Yeah," Motz said, but his heart wasn't in it.

NINETEEN

Shadows

As the brown Mercedes pulled away from the curb, Motz gave it a half wave and pulled out his phone.

Meike answered promptly. "What's up, Motz?"

"Dunno," Motz said. "Just had a strange experience with Ebeling's expert."

"I thought you two hit it off last night," Meike said, a hint of reproach in her voice.

"It's not that," Motz said.

"You want to talk about it?"

"He acted strange on Steinwerder," Motz said. "Making fun of the three dead Hasanis, like it was all a big joke."

"Maybe he had a run-in with them before," Meike said carefully.

Motz hadn't thought of that. "Maybe you're right, but..."

"But what?"

"He just showed me Mustafa Hasani's condo."

"That's a sealed crime scene," Meike said. "You can't just walk in and—"

"No shit, but our expert friend did just that." Motz tried to remember if Wolf had resealed the door.

"Why?" Meike said. "Forensics didn't find much, except all

those plastic containers full of Rainbow tablets."

"What?" Motz said. "When?"

"The Forensics report came in this morning," she said. "While you were on Steinwerder."

"Oh, right."

"You said he acted strange in the condo," she reminded him.

"Right," Motz said again. "He just gave me a guided tour of the place. Marble this, gold-plated that, it was unreal. Wolf knows way too much about Mustafa Hasani's home-improvement plans."

"Sounds like he's obsessed with the little prick," Meike said.

"Exactly." That was it. "After going on and on about how much money Mustafa had, he went on a rampage about how they're winning and we're losing." And I went along with the charade, he thought.

"Who's winning?" Meike said.

"The bad guys."

"Sounds familiar, doesn't it?" Meike had a smile in her voice now.

Motz shook his head. Sure, he was usually the one saying all that, but not like Wolf. "He wasn't just blowing off steam. He sounded like, I don't know, like it was personal."

"Maybe Hasani or Kaiser is blackmailing him," Meike said. "It wouldn't be the first time."

Motz froze. Meike knew a bit too much about his extralegal dealings with Willi Kaiser.

"You want me to dig deeper on Wolf?" she said. "ComVor doesn't have much, but sometimes databases leave shadows."

"Shadows?" Motz said, an uneasy feeling in his chest.

"Yeah, gaps in information that don't make sense individually," she explained. "When analyzed together, they can form a pattern that tells a story."

"If you say so," he said. Like most cops his age, he typed up his reports with two fingers.

"I say so," she said.

"What've you found out so far?"

"He's a widower with a daughter in college."

Motz got that uneasy feeling again. "When did his wife die?"

"Two years ago," Meike said. "Lung cancer. She beat it once, but then it came back."

"That's rugged," Motz said. It might also explain Wolf's addictive behavior and manic mood swings. "How's his clearance rate?"

"Off the charts. I've never seen anything like it." She paused. "He *has* had more than a few civilian complaints, but he seems to have sailed through all of the disciplinary hearings."

"Uh-huh," Motz said. Wolf could talk his way out of a paper bag, but he probably had less subtle ways of getting suspects to withdraw their complaints.

"His finances also look in order," Meike continued. "He refinanced a small house in Barmbek to pay for the chemo. About what you'd expect from an honest cop."

Motz nodded. At least Wolf told the truth about Barmbek. "Where does the daughter go to school?"

"Hochschule für Musik und Theater," Meike said. "She's enrolled in the music performance program."

Motz gripped the phone tighter. Meike was talking about the big concrete whale threatening the kids in the leaves of Alsterpark. It was just around the corner from Alte Rabenstrasse, where Mikey Kopperschmidt's body was found.

"I should say she *was* a student," Meike said. "According to school records, she dropped out two months ago."

Motz exhaled. So much for the Mustafa Hasani connection. "Okay, thanks Meike."

"Sorry I don't have more," she said. "But I'll keep my eyes open."

"For shadows," Motz said.

"Correctomundo," Meike said.

PETER SARDA

TWENTY

Fall Guy

When Ritter entered Ebeling's office, his nose was assaulted by a bitter stench. Ebeling was standing rather than sitting behind his desk. He looked nervous.

To his right, a bald scarecrow in a pinstripe suit was looking out the window with his back to the room. Something about his posture told Ritter he had never done a day's work, let alone seen the inside of a gym.

"What happened at the safe house?" the scarecrow lisped without turning around.

Ritter recognized the snotty old-money tone from press conferences. Althaus. The new Innensenator. Ebeling's new boss.

Ritter said nothing. If Ebeling was going to hang Ritter out to dry, he would have to do it all by himself.

Althaus turned toward Ebeling, rimless glasses flashing above a sharp nose and razor-thin mouth. He was holding a cigarillo with a nasty bend between his second and third finger. Ritter had heard rumors about Althaus and senate page boys. Nothing concrete, but persistent.

"Well, Herr Kriminalhauptkommissar?" Ebeling said to Ritter.

"No, Herr Inspektionsleiter," Althaus said to Ebeling. "You're in charge of the Homicide Division."

Ebeling nodded hurriedly. "Very well," he said. "This morning at four thirty-seven, dispatch got a call from Polizeikommissariat 35 in Volksdorf—"

"That's not what I asked," Althaus hissed. "What the hell happened out there?"

"I was just getting to that—" Ebeling sputtered.

Althaus turned to Ritter. "How about you, Herr Kriminalhauptkommissar? Can you tell me what happened in twenty-five words or less?"

Ebeling's eyes were pleading with Ritter to say no.

"Yes," Ritter said. "Somebody on the inside gave up a protected witness to the Hells Angels, who made good on their threat to kill her."

"We don't have proof—" Ebeling protested.

"That's more like it," Althaus said, looking Ritter over like a piece of prime rib.

Ritter's flesh crawled.

"So, you think we have a bad cop," Althaus said. "Is that correct?"

"We don't—" Ebeling started.

Althaus held up a hand. His fingernails were polished under the nicotine stains.

"It certainly looks that way, sir," Ritter said, fighting a gag reflex.

"Who are we talking about?" Althaus demanded, his eyes studying Ritter's face.

"We don't know yet," Ritter said. "All we know is the attackers knew the location of the safe house and when Laura Wesselmann would arrive. Two officers lost their lives trying to save her."

"Two police officers died trying to protect a cop killer?" Althaus said incredulously, like he was hearing it for the first time.

Ritter knew for a fact it wasn't the first time. Althaus had received a report the night before that detailed the whole sordid story—at least the version Ebeling wanted him to hear.

"How the hell did that happen?" Althaus said. The question was directed at Ebeling.

"It's a long story," Ebeling said carefully.

"Then make it short," Althaus said.

"Well," Ebeling began. "As you know—"

"Tell me something I don't know."

Ebeling stared at the green blotter on his desk, like he was making a difficult decision. Finally, he said, "Six months ago, Laura Wesselmann was allowed to escape from police custody."

"What!" Althaus said. "You let a cop killer go? That's crazy."

Ritter couldn't figure out Althaus' game. Just the day before, Ebeling had blackmailed Ritter into signing a confidential memo saying that he, Thomas Ritter, was the person who had authorized the escape. The recipient was Innensenator Althaus.

"No," Ebeling said. "I most certainly would never have approved such a reckless move."

"Then who *is* responsible?" Althaus demanded. "The dirty cop?"

"No," Ebeling said.

"Then who?" Althaus repeated. "Remember, you're in charge, Herr Inspektionsleiter."

"Yes," Ebeling conceded. "But I can't stop detectives from acting on their own initiative. In fact, your predecessor issued guidelines to the effect that we should encourage the man on the street to make his own decisions."

Ritter took a deep breath and exhaled slowly. It took a lot of willpower not to jump over the desk and beat the shit out of Ebeling. The bastard had just told the big lie. And there was nothing Ritter could do about it.

"Great," Althaus said, his voice dripping with sarcasm. "We know how that worked out for him."

"Be that as it may," Ebeling said. "We can't change the past."

"Who made the decision?" Althaus said. He looked at Ritter again. "Your lead detective?"

"That's not so important," Ebeling said in a disgusting display of generosity. "Anyone can make mistakes."

Althaus turned on him. "What the hell are you talking about! We just lost two police officers. A cop killer is on the loose. This is a catastrophe!"

"I know, I know," Ebeling said, like he couldn't believe it himself. "The idea was not entirely bad." He smiled weakly at Ritter. "Laura Wesselmann did lead us to that meth lab in Copenhagen. But, as you say, Herr Innensenator, look at what happened." He shook his head with fake sadness.

"No matter who made the decision," Althaus said, "I hold you personally responsible, Herr Inspektionsleiter."

"Of course," Ebeling said. Oddly enough, he seemed relieved.

Ritter was getting the strong impression that Althaus and Ebeling had staged this conversation for his benefit. Both seemed satisfied with themselves and the outcome of their little act. They were openly framing a lead detective for their own mistakes—and letting him know it.

■ ■ ■

After scrubbing his hands and face with soap and hot water, Ritter used hard paper towels to dry them.

Then he looked into the steamy mirror. A burned-out cop with haunted eyes stared back at him. A veteran who had been professionally castrated by criminals with badges. A nobody forced to compromise everything he believed in.

Ritter twisted the cold spigot wide open and stuck his head under icy water to cool his overheated brain. The pounding in his head receded with each thumping heartbeat. By the time it was down to his normal fifty-eight, he felt around for the spigot and twisted it shut.

Then he wrung out his hair. Holding onto the sink with both hands, he whipped his head up and down a couple of times, spraying the mirror with droplets of water. Too late, he remembered his neck condition. After whiplash, you weren't supposed to do things like that, but old habits were hard to beat, especially in times of stress.

When the room righted itself, everything was unpleasantly bright, but at least he didn't see the man in the mirror anymore. What he saw was the plan in his head. He pulled his turtleneck back on and hit the door.

The air in the hallway cooled his head some more. Walking into his squad's office, he saw that Meike was busy at her computer. "I need you to do a background check on Innensenator Althaus," he said. "Finances, known associates, physical movements in the past month, the works."

"You got it," Meike said, quickly shutting a strange-looking window that contained computer code. She didn't seem surprised by the request. Another window opened, this one password protected. "Ebeling got a head start on us," she said, pointing to the screen. "But he's *so* 1990s. Folders and subfolders and sub-subfolders. No audio tapes, let alone videos. But we can change that."

Another window opened. This one contained what looked like a tape recorder. Meike hit Stop, Rewind, and Play.

What happened at the safe house?

It was Innensenator Althaus fifteen minutes earlier.

"You wired Ebeling's office," Ritter said, feeling his face break into a big grin.

"On his orders," Meike said sweetly.

Ritter wanted to kiss her. "Trust the man on the street."

"Woman," Meike corrected him. They both laughed.

PETER SARDA

TWENTY-ONE
Miss Meike

Twenty minutes later, Meike wasn't laughing anymore. She was looking at surveillance photos of former Innensenator Mertens taken just before he was killed in a Herbertstrasse whorehouse six months earlier.

The first photo showed Mertens entering the Sex Workers United headquarters in St. Pauli. There was nothing unusual about that. The Social Democrat had been an outspoken advocate of legal prostitution, working closely with the union founded by a former domina to provide whores with health insurance, retirement insurance, and the like.

The second photo *was* unusual. A close-up of Mertens coming out of the SWU headquarters in a ridiculous pimp costume. If you got past the blonde wig, oversized dark glasses, and slinky red jogging outfit, Mertens' face was recognizable. He was wearing the same costume they found near his latex-covered corpse in the Black Room of Herbertstrasse 7b.

The third photo told the whole story. It showed Mertens the Pimp walking toward the back gate of Herbertstrasse. The timestamp put him at the scene less than an hour before his own gruesome killing.

At the time, Ebeling didn't mention the bizarre costume to the press, which was understandable given his closeness to the family of his old school buddy. What *wasn't* understandable was not mentioning the photos to the detectives investigating the killing. Why the hell were they locked up in his office all this time?

"Ritter," Meike said, zooming in on the photo. "You better take a look at this."

"Find something on Althaus?" Ritter said, walking up. He stopped abruptly. "Oh Jesus. That's Mertens."

"In full metal jacket," Meike said. "Just outside Herbertstrasse."

Ritter leaned close enough for Meike to smell hand soap. "Where'd you find this?" he said.

"In Ebeling's office," she said carefully.

Ritter stood up straight. "Son of a bitch! He withheld material evidence."

"It gets worse," Meike said. "The photos were in a folder with Althaus' name on it."

"What!"

"It looks like Althaus was spying on Mertens, and Ebeling was spying on Althaus."

Ritter exhaled loudly and looked to the door. "I *knew* Althaus was dirty," he said under his breath.

"And Ebeling found out about it," Meike said.

Ritter just shook his head.

She knew how he felt. Ebeling had that effect on all his detectives. And Ritter was the one who had to deal with him the most.

"How did Ebeling find out?" Ritter said finally.

"I don't know," Meike said. "I just know he stored the evidence on a flash drive." She pointed to the miniature metal drive sticking out of her computer. It had a Polizei Hamburg seal on it.

"Where'd you get that?"

"Like I just told you, I found it in his office."

"Ebeling leaves blackmail material sitting around his office?" Ritter's voice telegraphed disbelief.

"I found it somewhere else," Meike said, barely audible, even to herself.

"Where?"

"Don't ask." Meike trusted Ritter with her life, but the only way to keep a secret was to tell no one. After her little run-in with BND, she didn't want it getting around that she had broken into her boss's floor safe.

Ebeling being Ebeling, he had written the combination in a little leather-bound booklet with all his passwords and locked it in the bottom drawer of his desk. It took Meike all of ten seconds to pick the nineteenth century lock.

Ritter was holding a fist to his mouth. His shoulders were shaking.

"Care to share the joke?" Meike said suspiciously.

"Don't ask," Ritter said and burst out laughing.

Meike did the same. Sometimes, all you could do was laugh or cry. Laughing was better.

"I know you're going to take very good care of that stick," Ritter said.

"Oh yeah," Meike agreed. She snatched it out of the computer, pulled down the neck of her sweater, and placed the small piece of metal on the inside of her green sports bra. It burned a little, but it was satisfying to see Ritter's reaction. She knew he'd be thinking about that one for a while.

■ ■ ■

After Ritter took off to parts unknown—probably visiting that too-young girl-next-door of his—Meike switched off her computer, double-checked the USB stick in her bra, made sure her burn phone was still in her pocket, and headed down to the garage.

Fifteen minutes later, in the restroom of a JET gas station, she hit the one contact listed on the phone. Good thing she was wearing rain boots. Some fool had yanked the soap dispenser off the wall. There were slippery suds all over the tile floor.

Indigo picked up after three rings. "Hey, beautiful," she said in her hoarse voice.

Too much weed, Meike thought. Whenever she looked at Meike, her eyes changed from cobalt to baby blue. It wasn't that Indigo was one-hundred-percent lesbian, she was just "open" to "new experiences." Meike wondered how far that went.

"Hey, girl," Meike said in a sing-song voice.

At least Indigo was smart enough not to use real names. That was the advantage of working outside the box. The Computer Chaos Club attracted all the talent that hadn't been bought off by BND's off-the-books cybercrime division. CCC was in on the secret from day one. Meike wasn't fooled by the blue hair and nose rings. Her "subcontractors," as she liked to think of them, were smarter than anybody she'd ever met in law enforcement.

"So, what's up?" Indigo said. "Cat got your tongue?"

"No," Meike said, her hand cupping the phone. "I just need to be careful."

"Don't we all," Indigo said. "Don't we all."

"You were right about Mr. Big," Meike said, using the agreed-upon code word. "He's bad to the bone."

"What'd he do this time?" Indigo said, her hoarseness laced with contempt. Meike had told her all about the page boys, playing up the cash payoffs to the families.

"Worse," Meike said.

"Not over the phone," Indigo reminded her.

"Don't worry," Meike said. "Same time, same place?"

"Same old, same old," Indigo said.

The line went dead. Meike looked at the phone shaking in her hand. This was not like snooping on Ebeling. She had just crossed a very red line.

She yanked the SIM card out of the phone, smashed it on the wet tiles with her rubber boots, picked it up with some remarkably thin and coarse toilet paper, dropped it into the stained bowl, and kick-flushed the toilet with her boot. She would dump the phone in the Elbe River on the way home.

TWENTY-TWO

Mr. President

Laura Wesselmann got off on the loose suspension and steering of the primer-gray pickup, but it was the monster tires, V8 engine, and 4x4 transmission that really grabbed her. She'd spotted the squared-off F-150 down the road from Ohlsdorf Cemetery—and the fucking Polizeipräsidium.

She squinted up at the lights on the sixth floor. Ritter was probably burning the midnight oil looking for her fine ass right under his nose. Her cackle turned into a cough that resulted in a loud *splat!* of loogey next to one of the monster tires. The mechanical door lock was a joke. Hotwiring the ignition was E-Z-P-Z.

Now she was tooling along the B447, the abandoned Harley a distant memory. The sign up ahead said Schnelsen was just two kilometers away. She fingered the gun butt digging into her side as she admired the sharp creases and backwards POLIZEI patch in the rearview. It looked almost as good as the uniform she'd worn in her live-sex act at The Cage in St. Pauli. Man, that seemed like a lifetime ago. Many lifetimes. Lots of blood under the bridge.

The F-150 veered onto the offramp, like it was finding its way home. Schnelsen was another suburban shithole, like Squaresville.

It had taken her a good twenty minutes in the stinky restroom of that JET station in Ohlsdorf to get the sticky blood off her body and the smoke out of her hair and nose. The hand dispenser was too slow, so she'd yanked it off the wall and dumped the contents onto her head. After that, it was Sud City.

Good thing she'd hung up Heidi's backpack ahead of time. The dear departed sure came through when it counted. Her pack contained a fresh uniform, ammo clips, a pair of lace-up boots with rolled-up socks inside, and a plastic bottle full of Gatorade. Little Miss Girl Cop was even thoughtful enough to leave her ID card and wallet, which had a couple of fifties stashed in a "hidden" pocket. More than enough for more Gatorade and Marlboro Reds.

Laura pulled the monster truck over to the side of the road. Then she flipped open the hardpack, grabbed another Red, and fired it up with a big black Bic lighter she'd pocketed at the JET station. That was the killer thing about the uniform. People looked away.

She flattened the map on the wheel and squinted against the smoke. Lutz Kopperschmidt, the president of the Hamburg Chapter, lived on a street named Dorfteich. She'd been to the house once with Konny but didn't remember the way because she hadn't been behind the wheel. Besides, she'd been higher than a kite. She hoped Mr. President had some crank in his car. She didn't want to go into the house and deal with that bitch wife of his and her snot-nosed kids.

Laura refolded the map, tossed the flaming butt out the window, and put the F-150 in gear. The monster truck didn't even get a look from two fatso losers in matching two-tone parkas sitting on a rusty grated-steel bench at a bus stop, waiting for a short-ass bus while the driver drank coffee from a Thermos two blocks away. Up ahead was Dorfteich.

Laura steered the fat tires onto the small street and looked for the corner house. There it was, with a white picket fence and orange awnings. The "badass" president of the Hells Angels was just a soft *normalo*. No Harley or Peterbilt parked on the perfect lawn, just some fucked-up high-tech tricycle that had too many colors.

Laura pulled the truck to the curb and took out the map again, like she was looking for something. Actually, she was. Her exit plan. After she took care of business—and snagged some serious crank—she'd have to get the fuck out of Dodge, but quick.

■ ■ ■

Forty-five minutes and a dozen Reds later, a low-slung black BMW station wagon slid by the monster truck, its taillights going red in the rearview at the wimpy house. Bingo. Mr. Fucking President his own self.

Laura slid across the bench seat to the passenger door, opened it quietly, jumped down, and closed it with a slight click. Then she took out Heidi's gun, cocked it with another slight click, and walked quickly to the white picket fence.

In the driveway, Lutz was bent over, pulling something from behind the seat. When he stood back up, he was holding a plastic bag with bulging blue-and-white stripes. Laura wanted to laugh. Mr. President had been at Aldi like any other suburban breeder, while Bitch Wifey rode the paperboy in the master bedroom. What a loser.

Laura hopped the low fence with a scissor step, crossed the lawn, and met her target as he was locking up with a *beep-beep*. "Guess who, asshole?" she said.

Lutz spun around, eyes wide. Then he tried to cover his shock. "Oh, it's you," he said too casually. "You got a lot of nerve showing up around here."

"No, *you* do," Laura said and shot him three times in his beer gut.

Lutz hit the clover grass heavily, the Aldi bag crunching loudly under his weight. While he writhed in pain, egg yolk mingled with a growing pool of blood on the lawn.

Laura felt eyes on her back. She wheeled around with the gun, aiming it at the nosy neighbor behind the half-open door across the street. With her free hand, she held up Heidi's ID card and screamed, "Polizei Hamburg! Get back in your house!"

The door closed.

Laura turned back to Lutz and knelt down, one boot next to his big red face. "How's it going?" she said.

"Fuck you!" Lutz said, trying to spit blood at her.

Laura casually put the gun against his left kneecap and pulled the trigger.

Lutz screamed, holding his leg and rolling onto his side.

"Better?" she said.

He chewed his own lawn like a sick dog.

She put the barrel to the back of his right knee and squeezed off another round.

The renewed screaming was muffled by grass.

She grabbed Lutz by his overly styled hair and smashed the muzzle into his clover-filled mouth, breaking ridiculously white teeth in the process.

Lutz tried to say something around the barrel but just drooled pink fluid and made a gagging sound.

Laura emptied the rest of the magazine into his dripping mouth. Bloody skull fragments splattered clover.

■ ■ ■

The drapes on the kitchen window didn't move. Apparently, Bitch Wifey wasn't as dumb as she looked. Ditto for the neighbor across the street. But it was only a matter of time before some mouth breather in a colorful parka called 110. Laura had to get out of here fast—after she grabbed her vitamins.

With the thumb and forefinger of her left hand, she picked up Lutz's keychain from the sticky pool of blood. Yuck City. She found the fat black key and *beep-beeped* the BMW, which blinked and shot the door lock open with an audible click. She dropped the key, opened the door with her sticky hand—fuck it, she'd be long gone before the cops got her prints off the handle—and leaned across the mushy leather.

She popped the glove compartment. Inside was a sealed baggie jam-packed with colorful pills, like candy. What the fuck. Lutz was selling shit to kiddies? Why didn't he just sell crank like a normal biker?

Laura already had the candy bag in her hand when she saw what was underneath. Her heart skipped a beat. A second baggie, this one bulging with beautiful yellow powder. Yes! The real shit. "Come to Mama," she said.

She undid the zip lock with a practiced motion, touched the powder with the business end of the gun, and licked the barrel. Her tongue tingled with joy. It was crank alright—and completely uncut, for personal use. She dipped the barrel a little deeper and took a monster hit with a wet sloppy snort. It almost took the back of her head off. Damn, this shit was seriously good!

Her pulse shot through the low roof as the crank burned her throat. She rezipped the blood-streaked baggie and stuffed it into a cargo pocket on the side of Heidi's uniform pants. Her face was red hot as she climbed backwards out of the BMW and onto the driveway like a hyperactive spider. Heart Attack City!

She walked-ran to the monster pickup, her eyeballs bouncing around the neighborhood in search of dickhead gawkers. She was almost disappointed that there was nobody to shoot. Then she remembered the empty clip. *Don't go off half-cocked*, Konny used to say. She'd have to reload in the truck.

Laura opened the big primered door, pulled herself up into the driver's seat, bounced the gun onto the hard bench seat, and fired up the still-keyed beast. Then she pulled the big door shut, put the truck in gear, and roared away.

At the end of the block, she passed a parked sedan that wasn't there before. A beautifully restored Benz, clean metallic-brown finish, waxed whitewalls, glistening hubcaps, Hamburg plates. The old guy behind the wheel was staring at her with cop eyes. He held his thumb over two fingers that followed her like a gun barrel.

Shit! She floored it. There was only one place to go, only one place she'd be safe. The harbor. The monster tires smoked onto the B447.

The brown Mercedes didn't follow in the rearview. That was more than weird—it was creepy. What kind of cop just sat there like a perv and watched a girl cop slowly pump 9 mm rounds into some fuck on his own front lawn? And those cocked fingers, that was full psycho, the kind of thing she herself might have done. She cackled.

Fuck the Hells Angels and their stupid breeder cars. Fuck the cops and their stupid mind games. She was leaving this stupid town for good, flying high with enough meth to keep her engine cranked for weeks. Shit probably came from Copenhagen. She cackled again. Goodbye Squaresville, hello freedom!

TWENTY-THREE
Déjà Vu

When the Charger gurgled onto Dorfteich, the big orange sun was still holding its own against the pale new moon. The well-kept single-family houses and yards that lined the short block reminded Motz of his own neighborhood.

"There it is," Ritter said, pointing to the blue lights flashing at the end of the block.

Motz eased the Charger past a cluster of onlookers and up to the nearest squad car.

KHK Wolf was on the raised concrete porch, three steps above street level, in the shade of an orange awning, leaning a little too casually against a white support post, his usual cigarette in place.

Motz snorted and killed the engine. "Déjà vu all over again," he said.

The two detectives got out and stretched their legs. They'd been trapped in stop-and-go traffic for almost an hour. Road construction had choked off the B447, making it impossible to drive on the median strip, even with the blue light.

They'd used the downtime to discuss the dirty cop at the Präsidium. Meike hadn't been able to dig up anything actionable yet, but her database shadows were pointing toward the man on the porch in front of them.

Wolf had spent his last dime on his wife's unsuccessful chemotherapy, while watching the Hasanis use massive heroin profits to buy up the Hamburg Senate. That would make any cop bitter. Not quite a motive, but it was a start.

And then there was Wolf's bizarre behavior. Wild mood swings that suggested mental or chemical instability. Tasteless, aggressive jokes about bad guys who died badly. Excessive drinking without any hint of drunkenness. And access to a storeroom stacked to the rafters with confiscated heroin, cocaine, crack, speed, even Rainbow—not to mention shotguns.

Finally, there was Wolf's little lecture to Motz about "cleaning up" the city's worst gangs on the windy balcony of Mustafa Hasani's penthouse.

Ritter was more skeptical, talking about "guys in the trenches mouthing off," but he hadn't been there. Motz adjusted his black jeans and followed Ritter through the gate up to the porch.

Wolf threw his sparking butt onto the blood-soaked lawn and sauntered down the steps. "Another great day for Hamburg," he said. "Another scumbag bites the dust."

"Herr Kriminalhauptkommissar!" Ritter said.

"Aw, Jeez, lighten up," Wolf said. "You know whose house this is?"

"It's a crime scene," Ritter said sternly.

"Lutz Kopperschmidt," Wolf said, suddenly sober. His face darkened as he pointed to the hardened blood. "The so-called president of the so-called Harbor City Chapter of the so-called 81 Motorcycle Club." He spat out each "so-called" like it was burning his tongue. "The world is a better place without that asshole." He looked like he wanted to kick the body.

"What happened?" Motz said.

"Same as the other killings," Wolf said matter-of-factly. "Torture, head shot, overkill. The only difference is the caliber."

"No shotgun shells?" Motz said.

Ritter was putting on gloves as he stepped to the other side of the body.

"Not when the bullets are 9 mm," Wolf said. "Not when they're fired from a P6."

"Oh," Motz said. "We've got the gun?" That would be a new twist.

"Just a guess," Wolf said. "For all I know, it could have been a SFP9, like the piece on your partner's hip."

Motz squinted at him. How the hell did Wolf know Ritter packed a single-action H&K? Then he remembered. Wolf was Ebeling's boy. The boss must've mouthed off about Ritter's previous career with GSG-9 in Afghanistan.

"You think the killer was one of ours?" Ritter said from his crouch at the base of Kopperschmidt's skull. He was poking something metallic underneath.

"I'm just saying," Wolf said.

You're just high and can't control your motor mouth, Motz thought. What a mess. Thanks, Ebeling.

He turned away from Wolf and examined what was left of the victim's knees. It wasn't a pretty sight. "Lutz, Lutz, Lutz," he said. "You really know how to make enemies, don't you?"

Another strain of tobacco smoke, this one deeper and rounder, was competing with Wolf's cigarette. It was the coroner, puffing on his cigar.

"What're we looking at, Rudi?" Motz said.

"The victim was shot in the stomach and both knees before being shot in the mouth repeatedly," Rudi said. "The shooter let him suffer. If it had been quick, he wouldn't have bled out all over the lawn like that."

Motz thought he saw eggshells in the dried blood. Or maybe it was just the sunset playing tricks on his eyes.

■ ■ ■

"I still say it was a cop," Wolf said. "Look at that precision kneecapping. I almost wish I'd done it."

Jesus, Wolf, Motz thought. Get ahold of yourself. You want the whole department to know you've got a drug problem?

"It looks more like revenge for the four Hasanis," Ritter said. "We'll wait for Forensics, but there's no evidence of police involvement."

"Yes, there is," a uniform said, walking up from the street. "We've got a witness."

Motz saw alarm in Wolf's brown eyes. It was there for just a second, but it was there.

"Who are you?" Ritter said.

"Polizeikommissariat 24 in Niendorf," the uniform said. "Your boss told us to canvas the neighborhood."

"My boss?" Ritter said.

"He means me," Wolf said. "I was the ranking officer on the scene."

"Sorry," the uniform said. "I thought—"

"And?" Ritter said. "Who's this witness?"

"Guy across the street." The uniform pointed to another house with a picket fence and awnings. "He said he heard shots, looked out his door, and saw a uniformed policewoman."

"A police*woman*?" Ritter said, giving Motz a look.

"Yeah," the uniform said. "She identified herself as a police officer and told him to get back in his house."

"She *identified* herself?" Ritter said in obvious disbelief.

Motz couldn't believe it either. There was no sign of a shootout, just another brutal execution.

"That's what the witness told me," the uniform said.

Uh-oh, Motz thought. Maybe the policewoman was their dirty cop. Wolf's druggie smirk didn't make him feel better.

"After that, the witness heard more gunshots," the uniform

continued, consulting his pad. "When he looked out his window, he saw the policewoman jump into a quote unquote monster pickup and drive away."

"Monster pickup?" Motz said. Since when did uniformed cops drive their own vehicles? They changed clothes at their precinct. That was policy ever since the RAF murder sprees Motz heard about in Polizeischule. To this day, BKA issued reports about the "next generation" of left-wing terrorists. Uniformed cops were still considered at risk.

Wolf had "I told you so" written all over his face.

"Okay," Ritter said. "We need to get this witness together with a sketch artist." He took out his phone and speed-dialed somebody.

Probably his master's voice, Motz thought.

"Herr Inspektionsleiter?" Ritter said.

Yup, it was Ebeling alright.

Ritter waited a moment and then plunged in. "It looks like a policewoman may have been involved in the shooting."

"May?" Wolf said. "Like *Mother May I*?"

"Watch it, Wolf," Motz said.

Wolf threw up his hands. "Don't shoot, Herr Kommissar."

TWENTY-FOUR
Chaos Computer Club

The red Fiat 500 waited for the packed double-articulated MetroBus 15 to sway through the intersection. Then it made a hard left through the by-now red light, bumping onto the large round cobblestones of Schulterblatt, past the FC St. Pauli fan shop, under the squat iron railway bridge, and into the Sternschanze district, home to Hamburg's "autonomous" scene.

Of course, the inhabitants were anything but autonomous, taking whatever handouts they could get and stealing the rest. Their colorful get-ups turned into black hoods and bandanas every May Day. They celebrated by throwing Molotov cocktails at Meike's uniformed colleagues, many female, many in their early twenties. Meike knew because she herself had put in two years of riot duty like everybody else after graduating from Polizeischule. It was a rite of passage.

Up ahead was the headquarters of the permanent revolution. Built in 1888, the Tivoli Theater was rechristened "Rota Flora" by the Trotskyites who occupied it in 1989, the year the Berlin Wall came down. Meike never understood the timing. It was *so* over. Succeeding generations covered the once-elegant building with political graffiti and banners that favored hammers, sickles, and red stars. Meike's colleagues could have cleared the squatters in an afternoon, but the cowards in the senate wanted to avoid the inevitable looped footage of riot cops cracking drug-addled skulls and "experts" working themselves into a frenzy over a "police state."

Meike wrinkled her nose at some dirtbag doing his business against the side of the former theater. Somebody really did have to clean this place up. Despite his corruption, Innensenator Althaus wanted to do just that, calling for the city to "retake" Rota Flora, but that was just for his real estate buddies.

Besides, gentrifying the district would create a nontrivial dilemma for Miss Meike. She made a big distinction between Sternschanze's spoiled activists and the numerous small shopkeepers who had to board up their windows every spring. If the district was ever gentrified, there would be nowhere for her to do her "kitsch shopping."

It wasn't just anywhere you could find an original moss-green porcelain Melitta coffee pot with a matching porcelain filter on top like her *Oma* used to have. Or an anatomically perfect antique mannequin with just the right spiked collar, nipple rings, and junk jewelry. Or a vintage Danish ceiling lamp that belonged in a black-and-white science fiction movie. For that, you needed a specialty neighborhood.

Bumping the Fiat into a tight parking spot just vacated by an ad agency geek in a brand-new "backwoods" outfit, Meike spotted Indigo's white-laced Doc Martens on the filthy steps of Rota Flora. Above her dirty-blonde dreadlocks was a screaming white-on-black banner that covered half of the upstairs windows of the building.

CAPITALISM WILL END ANYWAY.
YOU JUST DECIDE WHEN.

The oversized finger was pointing at *you*. Next door was a lovely "Welcome to Hell" poster, a relic of the G20 conference some genius had chosen to host just around the corner. The hooded and masked Black Block rewarded that brilliant decision by throwing huge chunks of concrete at riot cops from the flat roofs of neighboring buildings.

Meike was about to toot her horn when a filthy ringed finger knocked on glass. She leaned over the passenger seat and was greeted by cobalt eyes smiling at her. She popped the lock, and Indigo's big boots stomped the floorboards, bringing a strong whiff of patchouli, reefer, and grime with them.

"What've you got for me?" Meike said.

"Glad to see you too, sister," Indigo said, displaying swollen gums that looked like an advertisement for periodontitis.

. . .

"You're sure they're his accounts?" Meike said. She wanted to roll down her window, but you never knew who was listening. Besides, she'd probably end up inhaling sour-smelling reefer smoke drifting in from the street.

Indigo flipped the decal-covered MacBook to face Meike. A death's head ring pointed to the name of the business owner.

"Silicon Alley GmbH," Meike read. "That's hardly subtle."

"Or illegal," Indigo said.

"But the Cayman Islands?" Meike said. "Really?"

"What, you a racist?" Indigo's baby blues danced mischievously.

"Oh please," Meike said. "We both know he's a scumbag."

"You can say that again," Indigo said, her irises turning dark blue, like storm clouds. "That fucker wants to destroy all this!" She pointed out the window.

Some "occupier" on the steps of Rota Flora was chugging vodka while resting on an elbow in a North Face sleeping bag smeared with something dark and organic. His mutt dog was licking the excess from his dirty gray whiskers.

Whatever, Meike thought. Althaus was the shared enemy. "Then we have to stop him."

"How?" Indigo said.

"Don't ask."

Indigo grinned and held up a surprisingly clean USB stick. "It's all here."

"You a mind reader?" Meike said.

"Nah, I just hacked your brain." The blue irises glowed light and dark, like a lava lamp.

Something cold ran down Meike spine. "You aren't wired, are you?" she said. The words just popped out. That was the problem with digital anything. It cut both ways. You never knew for sure if you were hunter or hunted.

"Never," Indigo said. "I'm no cop."

"Sorry," Meike said. "I had to ask."

Indigo shrugged and reached for the door.

Meike grabbed her scuffed leather sleeve. "Before you go," she said.

"Yeah?" The door clicked shut discreetly. It sounded almost intimate.

"No *MOPO*," Meike said. "Yet."

"Aw, come on," Indigo whined. "That takes all the fun out of it."

"For this to work, we gotta go dark."

"You mean *you* gotta go dark," Indigo said. "What's in it for me?"

Meike felt a hot hand on her right thigh. "One step at a time," she said. "We'll nail the bastard, but at the time and place of our choosing." My choosing, she thought.

Indigo's lower lip stuck out. "That's what you always say."

"We'll get the bastard," Meike assured her.

"That's not what I meant."

"I'll be in touch," Meike said, leaning into the leather jacket and unlatching the passenger door.

Indigo's eyes looked hurt enough for Meike to feel a slight pang of conscience. After the Doc Martens disappeared without another word, she pulled the door shut hard enough to feel it in her ears, hit the lock, and reached for the bottle of Sterillium Virugard in her jacket.

TWENTY-FIVE

Stowaway

Laura Wesselmann cut the lights of the F-150 and squinted into early morning fog. The big tires crept silently over the gritty wet concrete.

The sound of a shotgun blast made her jump in her seat. Then she realized it was just a monster container being slammed by a monster crane onto a monster ship. Still, her heart was pumping like a big bass drum. The meth didn't help. She had to cool it on that shit. For now, at least. Take care of business. There would be plenty of time for a tingly scalp later.

She looked down at the time she had written on the back of her left hand. She compared it to the shadowy hands on the clock tower shimmering through the haze. The point-to-point schedule on the Hamburg Süd website had said the *Polar Peru* was shoving off in less than twelve hours.

The Indian owner of the twenty-four-hour Internet café under the Steinbruck railway bridge didn't say shit when she flashed Heidi's ID card, her blood-encrusted bird finger over the photo. But she felt suspicion under that turban thing of his. He had some stupid six-armed idol goddess with barely covered tits on a pedestal behind the cash register, like that would stop 9 mm rounds to his hot black eyes. Fuck him and the cow he rode in on.

According to Hamburg Süd, shipping time to Mariel, Cuba, was thirty days, with no stopover in Mexico like the other freighters, so she'd gone back up to the goddess counter and grabbed all the dried food and bottled water the Indian had in stock, plus a jumbo pack of two-ply toilet paper and ten cartons of cigs. He didn't have enough Reds, so she had to settle for a couple of cartons of Lucky's. When he tried to give her shit, she shoved the big black gun in his face. The little prick threw in a handful of Bic lighters for free, just to prove he supported his local police.

Now it was a slow countdown to blastoff on the HHLA terminal on Waltershof. She put the F-150 back in gear and steered it between looming stacks of containers. It was dark as shit. No sunlight, no nothing, just more shotgun blasts that made her jumpy.

She almost hit the light switch but thought better of it. No sense attracting attention, even if the cranes were operated by robots. Some poor fucks were steering them from computer monitors in some control room. To see where they were going, they used cameras that could be pointed her way. There was no way to tell with all this computer shit.

That meant she had to rely on her meth-powered night vision. When that kicked in, she could almost read the white stenciled numbers. It took forever, but she finally found the right row and the right container.

She double-checked the number written on her inner forearm. It matched the massive corrugated-steel box in front of her. Home for the next month. She killed the engine, squeaked open the big door, and jumped down onto slippery concrete that almost took her feet out from under her. "Whoa, cowboy!" she said. Her voice sounded like it came from somebody else in the cold fog.

She walked to the back of the truck, stuck one of Heidi's boots on top of a monster tire, hoisted her sixpack stomach over the edge, felt around the truck bed without fucking up her hands too bad, and came up with a crowbar. The thing scraped the side of the truck and made a loud echoey clang when it hit the concrete. Shit. She looked around quickly but saw only foggy corrugated steel. Another shotgun blast told her everything was okay.

She carried the crowbar up to the big container door. She felt around for the lock, this time losing a chunk of knuckle before hitting paydirt. She grabbed the crowbar like a baseball bat and swung it up at the lock with all her might.

The loud crack kicked back painfully in her hands, but she somehow held onto the bar as it pulverized wet concrete at her feet. She reached with one hand toward the lock but couldn't find it. Then she spotted the hunk of useless metal near her feet. The crowbar had mangled that lock bigtime. She leaned the heavy steel bat against the left-hand door and reached for the latch on the right. Another knuckle bit the dust, but the right-hand door made a deep creaking sound. She pulled it open and stared up into stale darkness. Fuck that.

She marched back to the truck, hooked a foot on the monster tire again, flipped herself into the steel bed, and marched across spongy suspension to the toolbox that was right where it should be, behind the driver's seat. She slid its heavy ass to the back with three serious shoves. Then she jumped over the door and onto the bouncy bumper, unlatching the door and pulling it open on her way down to the concrete.

The bed of the truck was now at tit level. She reached over the open door, grabbed the toolbox by the handle, and scraped it toward herself with one motion, using her knee to guide it down to the ground. After exhaling a chunk of nicotine into the loud fog, she grabbed the toolbox with both hands and jerked it off the concrete and used the swinging weight to quick walk it to the container. She dumped it just inside the open door with a *bang!*

She flipped open the latches and rummaged around until she found what she was looking for. An industrial flashlight. She clicked the button in the middle with her thumb and was almost blinded.

Holding her other hand in front of her blinking eyes, she aimed the light into the container and saw mountains of full gunny sacks on pallets. The bill of lading said it was some kind of grain. Caribbean types probably weren't big on farming. Too busy drinking Coco Locos out of coconut shells.

She switched off the light, squinted at the sudden darkness, and stomped back to the doorway on the noisy steel floor. She jumped down onto the concrete with both feet, picked up the crowbar from its resting place next to the door, and dragged it back to the truck, where she heaved it over the side. She barely heard the clang over another shotgun blast.

She opened the passenger door and started grabbing the shit she got off the Indian. It took her six trips to get all the supplies to the container. The heaviest was the water—and the most important. Thirty days was a long time. It was hot down there in Coco Loco Land.

Satisfied with her work, she jumped back into the cab and drove into fog that was starting to get brighter. She parked a couple of rows down, hand-kissed the dash goodbye, and hotfooted it back to her container.

For a second she had a scare, looking up and down the row without finding an open door. Then she tried the next one. There it was. Whew! She wiped sweat from her brow. At least she could feel her biceps and pecs from all that lifting. Moving stolen goods sure beat working out at some pencil-dick gym in Eppendorf.

Now all she had to do was find a way to close the big door without letting the latch fall into place. She used pliers from the toolbox to bend some hard wire around the latch and twist that into a knot. Then she yanked on the latch a couple of times. It stayed in place. She was good to go. She stepped back into the container next to her shit and closed the heavy door behind her with a squeaky *bang!*

Damn, it was dark, even with a crack in the door. She used one of the Indian's Bics to find the flashlight again. The F-150 owner thought of everything. His flashlight was righteous. It even had a backup battery. She was *so* set.

■ ■ ■

Laura was jolted awake by a gunshot next to her head. The whole world was swaying. Her hand reached for Heidi's holster. Where the fuck was she?

She jumped up and put her eyes to the jerky crack in the container door. Outside, the harbor lights were moving at a dizzying speed. Another gunshot put her on her ass.

She jumped back up and ran to the crack just in time to see big block letters on the side of the hull.

POLAR PERU

"Yes!" she said. If Hamburg Süd knew what it was talking about, she was on her way to Cuba, not some shithole country that worshipped cows.

She decided to be positive. Like Konny said, it didn't get you anywhere to think shit might not work out.

Laura smiled at the memory of Lutz writhing in his blood on his fucked-up lawn. Konny woulda been proud.

TWENTY-SIX

Come to Jesus

While his bodyguards struggled to shove huge bundles of clothing into the oversized washing machines, Sulejman Hasani removed the handkerchief from his nose, studied the color of the fluid, flipped it over to the clean side, and turned another page of *The Prince*. He found the handbook for new monarchs as relevant to modern-day Hamburg as it was to sixteenth-century Florence. He had deep admiration for Niccolò Machiavelli's directness. It provided him with the counsel he sorely needed in these early days of his latest captivity.

> *There is no avoiding war, it can only be postponed to the advantage of your enemy.*

Hasani reread the line and underlined it with his No. 2 pencil. Then he resharpened the lead and put the makeshift weapon back in his sleeve.

> *It is a common fault not to anticipate storms when the sea is calm.*

He smiled sadly at the memory of his favorite passage. He had many favorite passages, but this one reminded him of his blind spot, the one that had put him in the hands of Milošević's hard men back in Kosovo.

The dark memory was overshadowed by the smell of laundry

detergent. His failure to anticipate storms when the sea was calm had brought him to this so-called prison. Compared to a Serbian concentration camp, it was a country club. But his failure to anticipate had landed him in captivity, nevertheless.

Hasani's quiet reflections were further interrupted by high whining and low thumping that filled the large concrete room. He didn't bother looking up. Obviously, his bodyguards had overloaded a washer again. They were simple country men, good for muscle but not much else.

They did not understand the complexity of power. The dialectic of thesis and antithesis that resulted in the synthesis of absolute rule. History was fate. What you did formed habits that formed character that determined destiny. The smallest details mattered as much as the biggest brush strokes. Everything you did and thought was forged into the whole of your character and its manifestation in the world.

Hasani paged back through the little handbook, revisiting other passages he had underlined.

Never was anything great achieved without danger.

Yes, that was very true, but the point about eternal vigilance was the key. Be bold when others are afraid. Be afraid when others are bold. The radical mixture of fear and boldness had kept him alive all these years.

Another passage addressed his current predicament.

An unavoidable war is called justice. When brutality
is the only option left, it is holy.

Putting out a hit on his equal in his enemy's organization had been the right move at the right time. He would have lost the war if he had responded "proportionally" to the killing of his three lieutenants on Steinwerder. He was a man of the East, not the West. Men of the West were not men at all. They thought war was some kind of game that followed rules. They did not understand that death was essential to life. The strong survived, the weak did not.

The men of the West had forgotten everything the master of war had taught them five centuries earlier. Machiavelli understood the necessity, yes, the holiness, of war. Conflict was always there. War was its resolution. The result, not the cause, was what mattered. Winning was everything.

After the infidels killed Hasani's nephew, he sent them an unmistakable message. But they mistook him for one of their own, one who did not think things through to the end. The fools responded with "escalation." They killed three nobodies, a direct affront to Hasani's honor as a warlord. That was intolerable. He had to cut off the head of the snake. It was his holy duty.

Hasani's meditations were interrupted by more loud banging. He sighed. His bodyguards had overloaded a second machine. Centrifugal force had driven the mass to one side of the drum, where it banged against the stainless steel with each revolution, causing the entire machine to rock on its feet. Now the two machines were rocking into each other, like giant robots dancing hideously on the prison floor.

Hasani glanced at his bodyguards. The two men were staring at the rocking machines and stroking their thick beards, as though hard looks could stop the drumming. With their bulk, they almost resembled the robot dancers who banged around the floor.

Hasani wanted to laugh, but something stopped him. An ancient fear, a trained instinct, an automatic response to something, anything, that did not fit. His damaged nose was on high alert, throbbing warnings of unseen danger. Something was definitely wrong.

The eyes of one bodyguard flew wide open a split second before the back of his head exploded, spraying the tattooed animal behind him with blood. The steel pipe smashed down viciously, again and again.

Hasani was behind the nearest machine in time to see his second bodyguard on the ground, fighting for a bloody shank on the polished concrete with another tattooed animal. The two rolled around in the blood. The animal was on top, his thick hands pressed into the bodyguard's throat. The bodyguard pressed his thumbs into the animal's eye sockets. The scream was drowned out by the heavy rocking of the machines.

The bodyguard managed to roll the animal onto his back. He used his full weight to drive the shank into the animal's left eye, where he twisted it. The animal's body jerked spasmodically, his boots slapping against the pool of blood. Then he stopped moving at all. Hasani had no doubt that he was dead.

That was when he felt a bolt of lightning in his left kidney. The bright pulsing pain followed his body as he turned and drove his sharpened pencil into the attacker's shaved temple, just below the tattooed snake. Hasani yanked out his weapon and felt around desperately for the shank in his lower back. He knew better than to pull it out, but he needed to hold it in place until he made it to the infirmary—if he made it that far.

The first animal was charging at him with the pipe over his head. Hasani stumbled backwards and tripped over the bloody mess he had just created. The animal landed on top of him with open eyes, blood spurting out of his mouth into Hasani's face.

Behind him, Hasani's bodyguard swayed heavily. Then he fell on top of them both, making the room go black.

■ ■ ■

The air was cool, the voices distant and somehow comforting. Hasani opened his eyes to near darkness. Above his head was a low, vaguely green ceiling streaked with weak yellow light that seemed to emanate from the voices. To his immediate left was some kind of beeping. Each beep emitted a red blinking light in the corner of his eye.

Hasani took a deep breath and tried to lift his head. He was thrown back violently. Something sharp and deep ripped into his lower back. Throbbing bolts of razor-sharp pain almost knocked him out again. He wanted to vomit. The room spun.

After the waves of nausea subsided, Hasani tried again, this time more carefully. First one eye, then the other. Slowly, the dim light came into focus. The beeping was more insistent now. The beating in his throat told him it was his own pulse.

He took a deep breath, held in the pain, and exhaled it out. After the seventh cleansing, the throbbing had beeped down to a tolerable level.

Very cautiously, he tried to lift his left hand. Something cold stopped his wrist with a metallic clatter. His hand dropped in fright. He was handcuffed to the bed.

He unclenched his right fist from the sheet and slid it down the rough fabric toward his pant pocket. Something sharp jabbed the back of his hand. The needle for the IV.

Looking down his arm, he saw no plastic tube. That explained the pain. They had not given him any morphine yet. He would make that work for him.

Cautiously, he moved his hand further down to his hip. He tried to reach for his pocket. To his horror, all he felt was flimsy material. A hospital gown. He shuddered at the thought of stumbling around Santa Fu in severe pain wearing a backless dress.

Something cold brushed against his right leg. He pulled back quickly enough to feel the jagged edge in his spine. He panted like a dog to fight the nausea. The fingers of his right hand touched something cold and rectangular. His brain did the rest. The raised bumps were keys. Someone had placed the phone where he could find it. Undoubtedly one of the guards on his payroll.

Hasani dragged the phone closer, doing his best to keep the top sheet from catching on the needle. When he could make out the keys, he used his forefinger to type in the number he had committed to memory three days earlier. The ring tone sounded like a weak mechanical foghorn, a stupid detail of civilian life he had forgotten. Nobody answered. After twenty rings, he hung up and tried again—and got the same result.

He hadn't felt so alone since Belgrade. Gunk from his nose was running uncontrollably down his cheek and onto the pillow. His left hand was useless. The hospital gown didn't protect him from the gnawing cold creeping up from the tile floor. There was no one to help him. He assumed that two of his bodyguards were dead. The third would have to empty his colostomy bag by himself.

Hasani knew that the next few minutes would decide his fate. With the resolve that always came to him at such critical times, he fought jabs of pain to focus on the keys as he punched them. When the ringing started again, he collapsed back into the pillow.

This time, he got the number right. After five rings, his ear was blasted by a tubercular cough at very close range.

He winced and cleared his throat. It felt like it was glued half shut. "Get me out of here," he said, shocked by the weakness of his own voice. Only then did he notice the tube in his good nostril. It smelled clean and cold. He must be in worse shape than he'd thought.

"Not my job," the voice on the other end drawled.

"Your job is to follow orders," Hasani said. "You do what I tell you to do. Or you will end up in here with me."

"Let's not get snippy, Sulejman," the voice said.

Sulejman. The drug addict policeman had just uttered his name on the telephone. Anybody could be listening. That was unforgivable. On the outside, he would have personally burned the bastard's tongue off with a blowtorch.

"You have one hour," Hasani said and pressed the big button. The phone slipped from his hand and down the pillow to the sheet.

"One hour, huh?" a guttural voice said. "That oughta be enough time."

Hasani's eyes jumped to the doorway. It was filled with a big, fat animal in a filthy clerical collar. Preacher. The Hells Angel was playing with rosary beads resting on his enormous belly. The tattoos on the backs of his thick fingers were flexing. "Greetings from Lutz Kopperschmidt," he said.

Hasani heard a strangled sound from his own throat.

Preacher smiled approvingly, carefully positioning the crucifix to face Hasani.

An ugly steel pipe appeared out of nowhere. Preacher slapped it against his thick palm. "Time to come to Jesus," he said, moving toward the bed with rhythmic steps. *Slap! Slap! Slap!*

Hasani hated himself for jerking the handcuff against the rail. There was no way out. He sunk back into the pillow and closed his eyes.

Searing white pain shot through his skull, sending it sharply to the right. Spitting out teeth onto the sheet, he saw his own blood splatter against the railing. More white pain exploded on the right side of his jaw, shattering molars. He choked on blood and prayed for death.

After an excruciating number of white explosions that slammed his head from side to side and filled his throat with more blood and teeth, he finally got his wish.

TWENTY-SEVEN

The Hunter

"I don't believe this," Meike said. "Wolf just took a call from Hasani on his work phone!"

She stared at her screen to reconfirm the unthinkable. There it was in black and white. Their big expert, KHK Wolf, had spent almost a full minute on the phone with the imprisoned head of the Albanian mafia.

"You're shitting me!" Motz said.

Meike felt his heavy footsteps on the carpeted floor. "It's right here," she said, pointing to the screen.

"How do you know the call came from Hasani?" Ritter said, striding across the room. "We confiscated all his phones."

"Because Wolf called him by his first name," Meike said. "How many Sulejmans do you know in Santa Fu?"

"Only one," Ritter admitted. "Sulejman Hasani."

"We've got our bad cop," Meike said grimly. "It was Wolf the whole time."

"Son of a bitch," Motz said.

"And he left an electronic trail," Meike said. "It's almost like he wants to get caught."

"Or he's playing with us," Motz said.

"Or that."

"When did Hasani call him?" Ritter said. "Exactly."

Meike checked the number against the clock. "Fourteen, fifteen minutes ago."

"Is this just the latest call?" Ritter said, pointing to the other dates on the screen.

"Yeah," Meike said grimly. "They've been in contact for three days. Ever since Mustafa Hasani was killed."

"That sneaky little fuck," Motz said. "I knew he was wrong on the balcony."

"What balcony?" Ritter said.

Motz didn't seem to hear him. "I should have listened to my gut," he said.

Ritter turned back to Meike. "Where is he right now?"

She checked her screen again. "His phone's been off since the last call."

"Which means he's on the move," Motz said.

Meike nodded. "He may be playing with us, but he's not stupid. Maybe the call changed his plans."

"Maybe his chart will tell us more," Motz said from the doorway.

"What chart?" Meike said.

"Something he told me about."

"When?"

"Hansa Stuben," Motz said. "I thought he was just talking shit. Fuck me." He stomped down the hall.

Meike was on her feet now, her chair shooting back from the desk. Motz was onto something. Something big.

"Hansa Stuben?" Ritter said.

"Tell you later," Meike said, running after Motz. She heard Ritter's footsteps behind her.

■ ■ ■

Meike studied the map on the wall while Ritter and Motz tore apart the rest of Wolf's office, like breaking things would speed up the search.

"His first name is Noah?" Motz said, holding up a case file with a signature at the bottom.

"Yeah," Meike said absently. "Noah Wolf." Something about the brushed stainless-steel frame of the map bothered her. It was sticking a good two centimeters from the wall. Normally, their maps were printed on thin posterboard. The bigshots with corner offices had back-lit Plexiglas. This one was different.

She touched the frame cautiously. It moved. She went with the movement, sliding it all the way to the left. What she saw made her stop. Wolf's "secret compartment" contained nothing but a white board. In the middle was a big smiley face drawn with a red marker. She laughed bitterly. Motz was right. The bastard really was playing with them.

"Find something?" Motz said.

"He knew we'd search his office," Meike said and slid the map back in place. "We're not going to find anything here."

* * *

Fifteen minutes later, the three of them stood outside Wolf's modest house in Barmbek. It was behind an old shoe-repair shop with the family name written in that retro paintbrush script Meike rarely saw outside of St. Pauli. Both buildings had well-maintained beige stucco walls, brown wooden trim, and immaculate double-paned windows. Both had deep shadows inside. It was impossible to tell if anybody was home.

"It's gotta be in the garage," Motz said. He was standing on his tiptoes to see into the small windows at the top of the brown wooden doors.

"Yeah, okay," Meike said. "But we've got to keep an eye on the house and shop."

"Do that," Motz said.

Ritter nodded, which made it an order.

The thatched butt of the P6 was slippery in Meike's hands. Adrenaline pumped through her veins, almost audibly. This is how it happens, she thought. She made sure the safety was off and walked sideways to the back door, careful to keep away from the dark windows.

"Looks like he uses it for his Mercedes," Motz said behind her back. He sounded disappointed.

A metallic crash spun Meike around, bringing the sights of her gun up to Motz's buzzcut. She pulled her finger away from trigger guard fast.

Motz was pulling the broken lock off the door.

Thanks for warning me, Meike thought. She turned back to the house quickly. Those few seconds of distraction could have gotten her killed. She put her finger back in place.

She didn't hear them open the garage door, but she heard Motz banging things around inside. A quick look over her shoulder told her the garage contained a well-stocked workbench, an ancient lawn mower, and a serious oil stain. She resumed her watch of the back door nervously. It was too quiet in the dark house.

"Son of a bitch," Motz said.

Meike felt something behind her. Ritter. No footsteps.

Motz clomped up behind him. He looked really, really angry.

"You hear somebody screaming inside?" Ritter said, his SFP9 aimed at the middle of the door, chest height.

"Oh yeah," Meike said and tightened her grip on her own gun.

Motz took two quick steps past them and kicked the lock with the heel of his boot. Brown wood splintered into the shadows. He kicked the splinters away and marched in, gun first.

Ritter and Meike followed.

They cleared the house carefully, room by room, their backs to each other. Living room. Kitchen. Dining room. Family room. Bathroom. Bedroom One. Bedroom Two. Clean, clean, clean, clean, clean, clean, clean.

All they found were two sturdy violin cases in a closet. Both were big enough to hold sawed-off shotguns and ammo. But that was a false alarm. Both contained violins, of all things. One had a lion's head instead of a scroll. No rogue cop blasted gunfire from the shadows.

Meike kept her gun at the ready and walked back into the kitchen.

Motz was studying a locked door next to an old fridge that was humming loudly. "This has got to be it," he said.

That's what you said before, Meike thought.

"Go," Ritter said.

Another well-directed kick ripped the lock from the doorframe. The door flew wide open and stayed that way.

Ritter followed Motz down the concrete steps. Meike did the same but kept an eye on the doorway. For all she knew, Wolf had been in the shop and had just entered the kitchen above their heads.

A loud click was followed by a flash of light in the doorway that made Meike hunch down on the stairs. The swaying shadows told her Motz had just pulled the string on a hanging lightbulb in the basement. She wiped her brow and forced herself to concentrate on the shadows behind the doorway. They had become even darker thanks to the light below.

"This you gotta see," Motz said in a muffled voice.

"What is it?" Meike yelled over her shoulder.

"Madness," Motz yelled back up at her.

Carefully, Meike worked her way down the rest of the stairs, her gun still facing the doorway up top. When she felt solid ground under her boots, she ventured a look over her shoulder. What she saw sent a shiver down her spine.

The walls of the basement were covered with newspaper clippings and photos and police reports. One wall contained nothing but file photos of bad guys, organized by gang affiliation and rank. The coldness in Meike's spine went from fear to something approaching admiration.

"It's Wolf's chart," Motz said, awe in his voice.

Even Ritter seemed impressed. "Your guy documented the entire organized crime structure of Hamburg," he said.

"Look at the Xs," Motz said, pointing at two columns of the chart with his gun.

Meike's eyes followed the squared-off barrel of his P6 from one photo to the next.

"Mustafa Hasani. Mikey Kopperschmidt. Manhar Hasani. Besnik Hasani. James Hasani. Lutz Kopperschmidt. They're all here," Motz said. "Somebody crossed out their faces with a red marker."

Meike thought of the smiley face on the white board in Wolf's office. She shivered again. From where she was standing, the pattern was clear. Hasanis and Hells Angels were being crossed out from the bottom up.

"Look at this," Ritter said. He had his finger on a top-level X.

"Sulejman Hasani," Motz said.

"What?" Meike said, walking up to them.

"Wolf crossed out Sulejman Hasani," Motz said. He sounded almost scared.

"He killed Hasani?" Meike said.

"That would be my guess," Motz said. "Sulejman Hasani. Wow."

"But they just talked on the phone," Meike objected.

"An hour ago," Motz said. "A lot can happen in an hour. Especially if this guy"—his gun swept the wall of photos—"is the guy making it happen."

Ritter had his finger on another photo, this one on the Hells Angels side of the chart. It had one red slash through it. "What the hell is this?" he said.

"Work in progress?" Meike said.

"Otto Schulz," Motz said.

"Who?"

"It says here he's the chemist for the Hells Angels."

"He's next," Meike said.

"It sure looks that way," Ritter said.

Motz stood back and surveyed both columns of Xs. "I don't believe it," he said. "The fucker actually told me about this chart. Do you believe that?"

"He told you about his hit list?" Ritter said.

"His forward-compatible hit list," Meike corrected him.

"Jesus Christ," Motz said. "Wolf's no bad cop—he's a hunter."

"A hunter with a detailed plan of attack," Meike said. She could feel the cold rage behind the chart. The photos were lined up on an invisible grid. The precision was scary.

"Wolf's rationing his rage," Motz said. "Following his plan. Step by fucking step. One execution at a time."

Meike knew how Motz felt. Wolf was doing something eight thousand cops, two hundred prosecutors, and two hundred judges couldn't. He was executing bad guys. And he was charting his progress.

"This guy has got some balls," Motz said, stepping up to admire Hasani's X.

"Maybe we can trace his movements," Ritter said.

Meike's boots made their way back to the steps. "Maybe we can," she said, aiming her gun at the doorway again.

. . .

"You can place him at the exact time and place of all the murders?" Ritter asked. They were back at the Präsidium, at Meike's computer.

"That's right," Meike said. She studied the GPS coordinates and times on the split screen. They were a perfect match.

Wolf was outside Restaurant Engel when Mustafa Hasani was beaten and shotgunned to death. He was at Santa Fu later the same morning. He was on the Alte Rabenstrasse jetty when Mickey Kopperschmidt was tortured and shotgunned to death. He was at U-Haft when Manhar Hasani, Besnik Hasani, and James Hasani were released from custody. He was at the container depot on Steinwerder when the three Hasanis were shotgunned to death. And he was in Schnelsen when Lutz Kopperschmidt was tortured and shot to death with 9 mm rounds.

"Jesus fucking Christ," Motz said.

"No, KHK Noah Wolf," Meike said.

"Where is he now?" Ritter said.

Meike switched the GPS program to full screen and started the trace. "It'll take a minute or two," she warned. "*If* he's turned his phone back on for some reason." In his shoes, she'd destroy the phone immediately, no question about that.

She stared intently at the map. After a few seconds, a flashing red overlay appeared. "We've got him!" she said. "He turned it back on." Why in hell would he do that, she wondered. He had to know they would track him.

The red overlay started with greater Hamburg and got progressively smaller as it zoomed in on districts and neighborhoods and streets. Then it hit her. "He wants us to find him," she said.

"He wants an audience," Motz agreed. "That can't be good."

The overlay became a flashing red dot, centered on an

industrial area at the edge of the harbor. They had a hit.

"Wilhelmsburg," Meike said. She pasted the street address into a directory and squinted at the result. "It's a pig-feed refinery."

She felt cold air on her shoulder and trampling behind her.

"We're on our way," Ritter said from the doorway. "Tell MEK to get down there on the double." Then he was gone too.

Their footsteps pounded down the hall.

"Be careful out there," Meike yelled after them. She picked up the phone, her pulse jacked through the roof. She hoped they weren't running into a trap.

TWENTY-EIGHT

Pig Feed

Noah Wolf's corduroy jacket flapped wildly in the wind. He forced himself not to look down through the steel grating. Instead, he shoved Otto Schulz across the landing to the next flight of stairs.

The big biker staggered at the third step, his braided ponytail whipping his shiny skull, but he responded immediately to another vicious gun butt to the kidneys. His balance seemed off. Maybe it was the cuffs cutting into his wrists. Or the bruises covering his surprisingly soft body.

Wolf had wielded the steel pipe expertly, avoiding the bones that would be needed for the final trek up to the top. *Practice makes perfect*, his old man had always said. And: *No work is ever wasted*. Wolf wondered what he would think of his son now. This wasn't exactly shoe repair, more like housecleaning.

Wolf laughed mirthlessly. His poor mother never would have understood. Then again, she had every reason to understand, after what cracker assholes like Otto Schulz had done to *her* mother in Theresienstadt when Adolph was in charge.

At the seventh landing, Wolf was wheezing heavily. He resisted the temptation to fire up another smoke, instead coughing phlegm into the wind. His eyes jumped to the gravel down below.

Everything began to spin. He focused on the horizon. Better.

A deep horn sounded in the distance. A mammoth container ship was being tugged up the Elbe by an impossibly small boat. Mountains of colorful containers towered over it in the midday sun. It was incredible how many steel boxes they stacked on ships these days.

With a final cough, Wolf slammed the gun butt into Otto's kidney again. The old chemist responded like a beast of burden to a bullwhip. His heavy, swaying steps shook the grating.

Not that Wolf felt sorry for the asshole. Otto cooked up formulas to poison kids. What kind of sick fuck would combine fentanyl with meth and sell it to unwitting music students with bright futures? It was a chemical roller coaster that simultaneously sped up and slowed down Sarah's nervous system, sending her into a two-month coma before it killed her.

Wolf hit Otto again, this time so hard that he landed on his face and started to slide down the stairs, his ugly mug slobbering streaks of blood on steel. Wolf stopped that nonsense by slamming the steel toe of his boot firmly onto the step beneath Otto's crotch. The chemist screamed into the wind and struggled to his feet. It wasn't easy with his hands behind his back. Wolf encouraged him with another kidney punch.

By the time they made it to the top, Otto was a mess, his braid hanging sideways across his swollen, blood-encrusted face under an eye that was bloated shut. He spat out a tooth that bounced off the steel landing.

Wolf slammed him against the wall of the silo. "Ever hear of Jimmy Hoffa?" he yelled. "You know, the *Ami* union leader who crossed the mafia?"

Otto's single open eye darted back and forth, apparently confused by the question. Of course, the bastard's pale blue eyes were never that intelligent to begin with.

Wolf grabbed Otto by the back of his greasy neck and forced his head over the edge of the silo. Down below, small brownish rocks were being rotated in what looked like a gigantic blender. The thing had to be a good ten meters wide. The massive blades were moving fast enough to force the rocks to climb the walls of the silo, forming an inverted cone in the middle.

"Hoffa got ground into dog food," Wolf explained. "Wet, not dry. They fed him into a machine like this one, turning him into Purina Puppy Chow."

Otto's neck jerked in Wolf's hand. Good. The asshole knew what was coming.

"Of course," Wolf continued, "the machine you're looking at makes pig feed."

Otto jerked around some more.

Wolf pressed his windpipe against the edge.

Otto gagged pink fluid into the swirling mix below.

"Go ahead and barf," Wolf encouraged him. "It will be part of your special mix."

Otto's flabby shoulders tried to shake themselves free.

Wolf kicked the back of his right knee.

The big biker went down hard, sending another wave of steel vibrations through the landing.

Better be more careful, Wolf thought. It wouldn't do for the damned staircase to come off before he'd fed Otto to the swine he resembled. Like the old man said: *Measure twice, cut once.*

Distant sirens pulled Wolf away from the biker. Sunlight blinded him for a moment. Then he saw the flashing blue lights crawling across the bridge. Much closer, something green and shiny was making its way through the maze of factory buildings. Wolf squinted. "Is it just my imagination?" he said to Otto. "Or is that a Dodge Charger down there?"

No response, just labored breathing from the sack of shit at his feet.

The inside pocket of Wolf's jacket vibrated. He pulled out his phone and read the name on the screen. "Motz!" he said. "What took you so long?"

Something *vroomed!* below. Wolf watched the Charger do a wide brodie up to the base of the silo, sending a cloud of gravel into the air.

"Don't do it!" Motz's voice screamed.

"You don't have to yell," Wolf said, holding the phone away from his ear. "Haven't you heard of an indoor voice?" He laughed loose some more dark phlegm that splatted onto the bloody mess that used to be Otto's face.

Down below, the driver's door opened and Motz jumped out, one hand at his ear. "You don't have to do this," he said, out of breath from all that driving.

"Do what?" Wolf said, kicking Otto in the stomach. The chemist's body jumped but collapsed back against the landing. Wolf hoped the sick bastard had enough strength to get to his feet. Lifting a dead weight like that would throw out his back again.

"We can talk about this," Motz said, now at the base of the stairwell. He seemed to be counting the stories he would have to climb to join them.

Something flashed in the corner of Wolf's eye. Off to the left, Ritter was doing some intense MEK shit, running sideways to the next silo like a cranked-up Navajo.

"Stop!" Wolf yelled, jamming his gun against Otto's bloody skull. He yanked the chemist to his feet with strength he didn't know he had. It must be the last reserves of adrenaline kicking in—or the uncut meth he had snorted in the car. He'd thought of using PCP, but that would have clouded his judgement.

Motz was stepping back demonstrably now, his hands at chest height, like *he* was the problem. "Okay," he said on the other end.

"I'm stopping."

"Nice try," Wolf said. "Tell that special op partner of yours it's way past Bedtime for Bonzo," Wolf said. "He's not *that* good a shot, not with this wind."

"It's never too late," Motz said.

"Don't bullshit a bullshitter," Wolf said. "Your words, Motz." He tasted bile. "We both know this is long over. I just have one more item to cross off my chart." He grinned despite his burning throat. "You *have* seen my chart, haven't you?"

"Okay, you're right," Motz said, walking backwards some more and holding his free hand to his forehead, probably to get a better view.

"So you like my chart," Wolf said happily. He turned to Otto. "Motz likes my chart. I told you he would."

"I didn't say I liked it," Motz said.

Wolf felt the meth hit the inside of his skull like a freight train. "What, you think a stinking piece of shit like this deserves to live?" He slammed Otto's head over the edge of the silo again and was rewarded by a retching sound. "You know what this asshole does? He poisons little girls."

"Tell me what happened," Motz said. "It's just you and me, Wolf."

"Cut the crap," Wolf said. "We both know half the Präsidium is listening to this call."

"You're right," Motz said.

Good, Wolf thought. Let them hear. "She had her whole life ahead of her," he said. "Her whole fucking life." The orange sky was moving around like liquid. He had to close his eyes to keep his balance on the platform. Please God, he thought. Don't let me fall. Not yet.

Helplessly, he felt Otto slip out of his grasp and collapse slowly and heavily. Reflexively, he pulled his boots away from the big disgusting heap.

"Who are we talking about?" Motz said.

"My daughter!" Wolf screamed. "Sarah."

"Your daughter," Motz said.

"She had so much talent," Wolf said. "Her life was just beginning. Did I ever tell you she performed a duet with a student orchestra at the Laeiszhalle?"

"Really?" Motz sounded impressed.

"That's right. Vivaldi's *Concerto No. 8.* The other violinist was an exchange student from Hong Kong. But my baby was the star." Something caught in his throat.

"Wow," Motz said.

"Yes, wow," Wolf said. "She was a star with a bright future. And this asshole killed her." He kicked Otto again.

"Who killed her?" Motz said. "Who's up there with you?"

"Otto Schulz," Wolf said. "You know, the last box on my chart."

"The Hells Angels' chemist," Motz said.

"You get a happy face for that one," Wolf said. "You paid attention in class."

"I saw his photo in your basement," Motz said.

"Hear that, Otto?" Wolf said to the mess at his feet. "You're famous."

"They tell me your daughter went to that music conservatory on the Alster," Motz said. "I've always wondered what it looks like on the inside." It sounded like he wanted to change the subject.

Wolf's rage spiked. "Did they tell you where she went after that? Did they tell you *that*?" He felt his own spittle against his cheekbones. He wiped it off with his gun hand.

"No, they didn't," Motz said. "Tell me about that."

"She went nowhere," Wolf said, seeing her empty eyes staring at the ceiling. "I know because I went there too."

"Where?" Motz said, turning his body sharply to the right. He was probably getting hand signals from Ritter. Or maybe it was the MEK vans, which were getting all tricky and turning off their flashing blue lights.

It didn't matter. Nothing mattered anymore. "I took Rainbow," Wolf said. "I wanted to find out where she was, how to reach her." He was breathing heavily now.

"I hear you," Motz said, turning back to the silo.

"You have no idea," Wolf said. "You're trapped in your own mind," he said. "You can hear the blood rushing through your veins. You can taste your heart pumping. You can smell the colors of your organs." He gasped for breath. "But you can't reach anybody else. You're trapped in your own nightmare. You can't get out. It's like a film that loops over and over, like a train to nowhere that never stops. Hell doesn't come close to that."

"That sounds rugged," Motz said.

"That's how my baby spent the last seven weeks of her life!" Wolf yelled into the phone, his eyes burning wet. "Forty-four days in her own private hell. And there was nothing I could do to help her." His shoulders began to shake uncontrollably.

A flash of light blinded him again.

He blinked back the burning. No doubt an MEK sight was aimed at his forehead. Time to get this show on the road.

He slipped his phone into the breast pocket of his coat without hanging up. He wanted them to have the audio for Internal Affairs. Then he kneed and pushed and shoved and kicked and shouldered Otto up to his full height.

Otto's fat head bobbed like a doll in the back of a car. A long string of gooey pink fluid hung from his chin.

"This little piggy went to market," Wolf said and flipped him face first into the side of the silo.

Otto's face left a wide trail of blood on the galvanized steel.

"This little piggy stayed home," Wolf said, using his knee and shoulder to force Otto's shoulders up and over the edge.

Otto made more gagging noises.

"This little piggy had roast beef," Wolf said, forcing Otto's big stomach up and over.

Otto belched a hideous stream of vomit into the swirling rocks below.

"This little piggy had none," Wolf said, pushing Otto's fat butt up to the top.

The biker's shoulders and legs were flailing now, like he was drowning.

It was all Wolf could do to keep the fat fuck teetering in place so he could get a final close-up of his immediate future.

After taking a deep breath, Wolf secured his hold on Otto's greasy belt and hard crackly jeans. "And *thiiiis* little piggy cried *wee wee wee* all the way home," he said, pushing the rest of Otto over the edge.

The biker went head over heels into the swirling brown rocks, landing on his face and flopping around frantically as the circular current carried him around and around the wide silo. Good luck, asshole, Wolf thought.

Then Otto's shoulders were under the thick, rough surface, his skull glistening against the force that was pulling it down. Then it was swallowed by the mass of rocks swirling around the big tank.

"Wolf!" Motz screamed in the phone. "Talk to me."

"Yeah, I'm here," Wolf said. He turned around, stepped over to the railing, and waved, a big grin on his face. A creepy crawly spider of MEK guys with shields was making its way over to Motz.

Wolf laughed. It was ridiculous. He holstered his gun and straightened his jacket. Showtime.

Holding onto the hot railing, he focused on the orange horizon. The big container ship had docked at the HHLA terminal.

A robotic crane was starting to unload the colorful containers like children's toys. *This little piggy went to market. This little piggy stayed home.* The sun was burning Wolf's face pleasantly. Imagine that. Getting a sunburn with all the little piggies in Wilhelmsburg.

Wolf whipped his right leg over the railing. Then his left. He didn't feel the height anymore, just the irresistible golden horizon calling him home. He closed his eyes and let go of everything, floating, floating, floating into the wonderful warmth.

"Don't do it!" his jacket said.

But Vivaldi was already in the air. On Sarah's cue, Wolf lifted his violin dramatically. Together, father and daughter played the joyful music, swirling through the lush meadow. He threw her into the bright blue sky, only to catch her in his arms effortlessly. Together, they danced through the weightless clouds into eternity.

Epilogue

"You're saying it wasn't a real war?" Meike said, shielding her eyes. The sun spanned the mouth of the Elbe River, blanketing the entire harbor with an orange glow.

"That's right," Ritter said at her side. "Our late colleague, KHK Noah Wolf, manufactured it."

The two of them were sitting on the hood of Motz's Charger. The owner was standing with his eyes closed, basking in the orange warmth, a squat brown bottle of Flensburger in his big paw.

"But the Hasanis and Hells Angels hate each other," Meike said, taking another nip of her beer.

"They do now," Ritter said with a laugh. "That was Wolf's doing."

"What about Rainbow?" Meike said. "That definitely wasn't Wolf's doing."

"Rainbow was concocted by Otto Schulz," Motz said, his eyes still closed. "The Hells Angels' chemist."

"How do you know?" Ritter said.

"Because Wolf told me out there," Motz said. "He had no reason to lie. It was like a deathbed confession."

Meike nodded. Even on tape, it was obvious that Wolf was telling the truth. The story about his daughter was heart-wrenching.

Ritter frowned. "Otto Schulz was behind it all?"

"Yeah," Motz said, opening his eyes. "Rainbow was his brainchild. Mikey Kopperschmidt and Mustafa Hasani were his mules."

"Wait a minute," Meike said. "Why would Mustafa Hasani sell drugs for a rival gang?"

"Because he was a selfish little shit," Motz said. He took a swig of beer. "His uncle was safely behind bars for life. He saw a once-in-a-lifetime opportunity he couldn't pass up."

"Selling Rainbow to university students," Meike said, finishing the thought. She had to admit there was some twisted logic to it.

"Blame it on the new HafenCity campus," Motz said.

Meike nodded. "And the HafenCity coeds."

"And that," Motz said. "He gave them what they wanted. They gave him what he wanted. Everybody was happy." His grin went south. "Except the kids who ended up in ICU."

"Like Wolf's daughter," Meike said. "Sarah."

"Exactly."

"And Sulejman Hasani didn't like that," Ritter said.

Motz shook his head. "Hasani didn't know about Mustafa's extracurricular activities," he said. "Wolf just did what Hasani would have done if he had known."

Meike had to think about that one.

"But Hasani's enforcer found out before that," Ritter said. "Which is why he and his so-called associates kicked Mustafa down the stairs of Restaurant Engel."

"Yup," Motz said. "Wolf must have tailed Mustafa to Teufelsbrück. When he saw the Hasanis disciplining the little shit, he improvised."

"It was brilliant, when you think about it," Meike said.

Motz nodded. "That's what got Sulejman Hasani killed in Santa Fu. The Hells Angels thought he was interfering with their new business."

"And the whole time, Hasani didn't have a clue," Meike said. "Wolf played him perfectly. Forensics even found his business card under Hasani's bunk in Santa Fu." Man, she sure wouldn't want Wolf for an enemy, even if he was dead.

"That explains Hasani's call to Wolf from the infirmary," Ritter said.

"Exactly," Meike said. "Wolf wanted to toy with him one more time, like a cat with a mouse." She shuddered at her own words.

"There *is* justice after all," Motz said and raised his bottle. "Here's to justice."

Meike hesitated, then raised her own. "To justice."

Ritter did the same, but his mind seemed to be elsewhere.

■ ■ ■

"Wolf tried everything," Meike said. "Smell therapy, pressure therapy, music therapy, you name it."

"How do you know all this?" Motz said.

"I interviewed two ICU nurses at Krankenhaus Jerusalem," Meike said. "While you guys were in Wilhelmsburg cleaning up." After Wolf took a header off that silo. She was glad she hadn't seen it. She had just heard a rush of air on the wire. Then nothing.

Those intimate moments, when Wolf told Motz about his daughter—and the horrible silence that followed—really got to her. She had to find out who Noah Wolf, the man, was.

She found out. He was a father first and a cop second. The cop in him took over when the father in him was crushed. A good cop who did the right thing in the wrong way.

"They told me his grandparents were in Theresienstadt," Meike said. "You know, the SS ghetto in Czechoslovakia."

For once, Motz was at a loss for words.

"What happened?" Ritter said quietly.

Meike took a deep breath. "They were in the camp string quartet.

One played violin, the other cello, I forget which."

"They did what they had to do to survive," Ritter said. "They made themselves indispensable to their enemies."

"It didn't last," Meike said. "After the international press went back home, the Goldbergs—that was their name—got shipped off to Auschwitz."

Motz sighed heavily but still said nothing.

"That would explain Sarah Wolf's musical talent," Ritter said. "The violin, I mean."

Meike nodded. "The grandparents' daughter—Wolf's mother—managed to hide from the Gestapo in a shoe-repair shop in their Barmbek neighborhood."

"The other shoe drops," Motz said.

"So to speak," Meike said. "Anyway, at great risk to themselves, the owners took care of Wolf's mother for three long years." Meike smiled. "During that time, she fell in love with the shoemaker's son. When she got pregnant, they were married in a quiet ceremony. They named their son Noah, after his grandfather."

"Now it all makes sense," Motz said.

"It does?" Meike said. "It just seems so sad and tragic." She blinked back a tear.

"Yes, it does," Motz said, his eyes lost in the direction of Wilhelmsburg. "You should have heard him up there."

"I heard it on—" Meike started.

"Such a talented kid with such a brilliant future," Motz said. His eyes hardened. "And that lowlife Mustafa Hasani poisons her."

"We don't know it was Mustafa," Ritter said.

Meike wiped her eyes and nose angrily. Sarah Wolf looked like such a nice girl in the photos. What a waste.

"We know Mustafa was behind it," Motz said. "Many of the Rainbow zombies were students at HafenCity University."

"Sarah Wolf attended the Hochschule für Musik und Theater," Meike said mechanically. Like it mattered.

"Wolf wanted to find out where she was." Motz paused. "He said it was hell."

"And that two years after his wife's death," Meike said.

"Son of a fucking bitch," Motz said and threw his bottle into the Elbe.

Meike followed suit, as did Ritter.

Overhead, a seagull complained mournfully.

. . .

"Whatever happened to Laura Wesselmann?" Motz said.

The three of them were standing together now at the edge of the Elbe, swaying to a breeze that ruffled the surface of the oily water. The foghorn of a huge container ship honked like a lonely goose in the distance.

"Forensics found her bloody prints inside Lutz Kopperschmidt's car," Ritter said.

Meike chided herself. She had been too preoccupied with Wolf's daughter to even check. That reminded her. She took out her phone and paged through the headlines quickly. There was nothing but a bank robbery, somebody getting pushed in front of an S-Bahn, and some oldsters falling prey to a financial fraud scheme. She reminded herself to be patient. It wasn't time yet.

"What?" Motz said. "Laura Wesselmann killed Lutz Kopperschmidt? I thought that was Wolf."

"Well, the prints and ballistics point to her," Ritter said. "A 9 mm round found in one of Lutz Kopperschmidt's knees came from a P6 registered to the policewoman killed at the safe house in Bergstedt."

"By the Hells Angels," Meike said, putting away her phone. Or did Laura Wesselmann do that too? Meike didn't put anything past the little psycho.

"As far as we know," Ritter said. "Forensics is still sorting through that mess."

"What we do know is that Wolf was the first on the scene at Lutz Kopperschmidt's house," Motz said. "He could have been the killer."

"That doesn't explain Laura Wesselmann's prints," Ritter said.

"No," Motz said. "But we know Wolf was there before anybody else. What the hell was he doing in Schnelsen? His beat was St. Pauli."

"Don't forget the eyewitness," Ritter said.

"I thought the composite drawing was inconclusive," Motz said. "It could have been just about anybody in that uniform."

"Exactly," Ritter said. "Someone dressed like a policewoman identified herself at the crime scene while the murder was in progress. And she drove away in a monster truck. That sounds like our psycho friend."

"It sure does," Meike said. "She's crazy enough to pull a stunt like that in broad daylight. It wouldn't be the first time."

Motz shrugged. "You guys know her better than I do."

"Anyway," Ritter said, "Europol just put her on its most wanted list."

"In that case, her ass is grass," Motz said with a laugh.

"I wouldn't be too sure," Ritter said, looking at the choppy water. "My gut tells me she's already on her way out of the country."

An air horn echoed across the Elbe. Meike made out the name *POLAR PERU* stenciled on the hull of a massive container ship. It was flying a Cuban flag.

"For all I know, she's on that ship," Ritter said.

Something told Meike he might be right.

Motz laughed again.

"What's so funny about that?" Meike said suspiciously.

"Innensenator Althaus has got some explaining to do," Motz said. "First his archrival gets killed in a whorehouse. Then the killer gets away—twice."

Ritter was still staring at the water glumly. A seagull had just dropped from the sky and scooped up a fish swimming too close to the surface. The poor thing wriggled in its beak helplessly.

"Don't worry, Althaus will get his," Meike said.

"You care to share?" Motz said.

"Need to know." Meike hoped she hadn't just jinxed her own plan. *Don't count your chickens before they're hatched.*

"It must be something good," Motz said.

"Oh yeah," Meike said. If everything went according to plan. She rechecked her phone. Eighteen hundred on the dot. Her breath caught. *MOPO* had a new screaming headline.

Top Cop Linked to Albanian Mafia!

"Yes!" Meike said, her rubber boots slapping the dock for joy.

"That doesn't sound very need-to-know," Motz said. "Now you have to tell us."

Ritter's face was one big question mark.

Meike began reading out loud.

> *According to digital evidence provided exclusively to this newspaper, Innensenator Althaus, the top cop in Hamburg, is involved in money laundering for an Albanian drug cartel through a straw man company. Offshore accounts on the Cayman Islands registered to the Innensenator record wire transfers from Sulejman Hasani, a convicted heroin importer and cop killer, who was serving a life sentence when he was killed under mysterious circumstances in the Fuhlsbüttel Correctional Facility, commonly known as Santa Fu. Prison officials say—*

"My God, Meike!" Ritter said. He looked like he wanted to kiss her.

"We got the bastard," she said, feeling a wave of pride.

"How the hell did you pull that off?" Motz said.

"That would be telling," Meike said with a giggle.

"The state prosecutor is going to have a hard time *not* throwing the book at Althaus now," Motz said.

"I'm sure Ebeling will insist on it," Meike said, winking at Ritter. She had seen Ebeling's file on the state prosecutor. The Ice Queen had slept her way to the corner office, not knowing that at least one of her elderly benefactors was an exhibitionist with a hidden camera. Meike had seen the tapes.

It was amazing what Ebeling kept in his floor safe. Like the Althaus blackmail photos, she had put the hot video of the Ice Queen back after making a copy. Meike smiled to herself. Amateurs stole, professionals borrowed.

Ritter was grinning ear to ear and shaking his head. "I don't believe it," he said.

"Believe it," Meike said. "Ebeling will make Althaus responsible for his own mistakes, including Laura Wesselmann."

Ritter stopped grinning, like he was doing the math. Then he exhaled loudly.

"Ebeling's a political shark," Meike said. "And the sharks are going to have a feeding frenzy. Before they're done, they'll be biting themselves."

"I'll drink to that," Motz said, raising his bottle to the sunset.

The three detectives clinked bottles and emptied them with one go. Then they threw them into the Elbe. *Plunk, plunk, plunk.*

The seagull circling overhead didn't complain this time. It was more interested in the container ship steaming out of the harbor into the big orange sun.

List of characters

Dietmar ("Motz") Beck
>Bad-tempered homicide detective with deep scars. Born and raised in St. Pauli bar. Drives Harley and vintage cars taken from impound. Close to local gangster Willi Kaiser. Archenemy of Sulejman Hasani, who killed his former partner.

Dr. Dr. Rüdiger ("Rudi") Deichmann
>Cigar-chomping coroner. Cross between grandfather and butcher. First "Dr." is for internal medicine, second for pathology. "Rudi" is for tenure as coach of prison soccer team.

Dr. Klaus Ebeling
>Head of Homicide Division. Blue blood from old Hanseatic trading family. Adapts to shifting winds at City Hall. Political animal with convenient memory lapses.

Thomas Ritter

Lead homicide detective haunted by Internal Affairs as well as his boss, Klaus Ebeling. Former special operator in Afghanistan and Frankfurt for whom violence is reflex. Arrested Sulejman Hasani and Laura Wesselmann.

Meike Voss

Voluptuous homicide detective. Daughter of dock worker. Weakness for computer hackers and male coworkers.

KHK Wolf

Burned-out narcotics agent with his own drug problem. Expert on local gang structures. Called in by Klaus Ebeling to help investigate war between drug cartels.

CRIMINALS

Mustafa Hasani

Sulejman Hasani's favorite nephew. Graduated from courier to drug dealer when uncle sent to prison. Sells "Rainbow" to coeds at HafenCity University. Close to Mikey Kopperschmidt.

Sulejman Hasani

Albanian mafia boss serving life sentence in Santa Fu prison for killing cop and torturing another. Allied with Innensenator Althaus. Archenemy of Willi Kaiser, Preacher, and Motz Beck.

Wilhelm ("Willi") Kaiser

Old-school "King of St. Pauli." Rules red-light district with iron fist. Took over bar from Motz Beck's father in return for "protection." Subcontracts out enforcement work to Hells Angels. Archenemy of Sulejman Hasani.

Konny

Laura Wesselmann's former cellmate. Killed by Danish police in raid of meth lab at farmhouse outside Copenhagen.

Lutz Kopperschmidt

President of Harbor City Chapter of Hells Angels. Controls crystal meth trade in Hamburg. Put out hit on Laura Wesselmann after she testified against Copenhagen Chapter.

Mikey Kopperschmidt

Prospect of Harbor City Chapter of Hells Angels. Half-brother of Lutz Kopperschmidt. Middleman between Otto Schulz and Mustafa Hasani.

Preacher

Oversized enforcer for Harbor City Chapter of Hells Angels inside Santa Fu prison. Wears dirty clerical collar and robe over tattoo-covered body. Conducts "Come to Jesus" meetings with steel pipe. Archenemy of Sulejman Hasani.

Otto Schulz

Chemist of Harbor City Chapter of Hells Angels who concocted "Rainbow," colorful tablets containing fentanyl and methamphetamine for sale to upper-class students.

Laura Wesselmann

Cop killer turned state's witness after inadvertently leading Europol to Hells Angels meth lab at farmhouse outside Copenhagen. Former cellmate of Konny.

POLITICIANS

Hans-Dieter Althaus

> New Innensenator who wants to tear down St. Pauli whorehouses and transform district into high-tech business park called "Silicon Alley." Secret real-estate ties to Sulejman Hasani.

Carsten Mertens

> Former Innensenator killed in St. Pauli S&M room by Laura Wesselmann. Wanted to protect whorehouses from closure by Hans-Dieter Althaus. Close to Willi Kaiser.

List of terms

Black Block

Group of violent demonstrators who wear black clothing and bandanas to hide identities from police. Meike Voss despises group, which attacked her female colleagues in anti-G20 rioting.

BND

Bundesnachrichtendienst. Federal Intelligence Agency. German equivalent of CIA. Database was penetrated by hacker at request of Meike Voss, who was investigating Thomas Ritter.

breeders

Derogatory slang for heterosexuals. Laura Wesselmann's term for people with children.

Bundeswehr

United military force of Germany. Established in 1950. Motz Beck, Thomas Ritter, and Sulejman Hasani have deep—and conflicting—ties to Bundeswehr.

Cage, The

Live-sex theater in St. Pauli. Former machine factory with iron cage for female "combatants." Former workplace of Laura Wesselmann.

Casino Esplanade

Casino owned by Sulejman Hasani, who laundered money from penthouse office overlooking blackjack tables. Scene of confrontations between Motz Beck, Thomas Ritter, and Hasanis.

CCC

Chaos Computer Club. Hacker organization infiltrated by Meike Voss to gather dirt on Innensenator Althaus.

ComVor

Database for tracking police officers. As Meike Voss discovered, Thomas Ritter's record is sealed because of his covert work for GSG-9 in Afghanistan.

Drogendezernat

Narcotics Division (LKA 68). Formal name of drug squad to which KHK Wolf belongs.

EU

European Union. Political and economic union of 27 member states located primarily in Europe, with estimated total population of about 447 million people.

Europol

European Union Agency for Law Enforcement Cooperation. Law enforcement agency of EU formed in 1998 to handle criminal intelligence and combat serious international organized crime and terrorism through cooperation between EU member states.

Fischmarkt

Fish market on Elbe River. Where night owls and early birds barter for fresh fish every Sunday morning. Rendezvous point for Thomas Ritter, Motz Beck, and Meike Voss.

fish-head

Fischkopp. Slang for person from Northern Germany, particularly Hamburg.

GSG-9

Grenzschutzgruppe 9. Border Protection Group 9 of Federal Police. As member, Thomas Ritter conducted joint operations with FBI in Afghanistan in 2001.

Hafenkrankenhaus

Port hospital in St. Paul founded in 1900 as police hospital. Motz Beck was treated there at age 16 after getting hit over head with motorcycle chain by future president of local Hells Angels, Lutz Kopperschmidt.

Herbertstrasse

Legendary gated street in St. Pauli with wall-to-wall whorehouses. Where former Innensenator Mertens was killed.

Innensenator

Senator for Interior. Ultimate boss of Polizei Hamburg. Hans-Dieter Althaus took position after his archrival, Carsten Mertens, was killed by Laura Wesselmann in whorehouse.

Inspektionsleiter

Chief of Detectives. Rank held by Klaus Ebeling, who heads Homicide Division.

KHK

Kriminalhauptkommissar. Lead Detective. Rank held by Ritter and Wolf.

KOK

Kriminaloberkommissar. Detective. Rank held by Motz Beck and Meike Voss.

LKA

Landeskriminalamt. State Criminal Investigation Office. Polizei Hamburg is responsibility of *Innensenator*. Klaus Ebeling, Thomas Ritter, Motz Beck, and Meike Voss belong to LKA 411 (Homicide). KHK Wolf belongs to LKA 68 (Narcotics).

MEK

Mobileinsatzkommando. Mobile deployment command. German equivalent of SWAT. Similar to Thomas Ritter's SEK in Frankfurt. Commandos from MEK unit storm pig feed refinery.

moin

Low German greeting common in Northern Germany, particularly in working-class districts like St. Pauli. Can be used any time of day.

MOPO

Hamburger Morgenpost. Local tabloid with screaming headlines that are usually accurate. Secondary source of news for residents of St. Pauli. Primary source is extensive rumor mill.

Mordkommission

Homicide Division. Designates homicide squads, like that formed by Thomas Ritter, Motz Beck, and Meike Voss. Polizei Hamburg has six such squads.

Motz

Nickname for Dietmar Beck derived from "*motzen*," which means to complain. On seeing nickname, Thomas Ritter knows his new partner is complainer.

normalos

Normal people who do not exhibit particularly deviant characteristics or behaviors. One of Laura Wesselmann's less offensive terms for people unlike herself.

P6

SIG Sauer P6. Standard handgun used by Hamburg police officers like Motz Beck and Meike Voss. Variant of P225, which has tighter trigger pull.

POLAS

Police Information System. Police database used to track criminals. Meike Voss uses database to connect Sulejman Hasani and Willi Kaiser with known associates.

Polizeipräsidium

Police headquarters. Footprint of mammoth building in Winterhude matches twelve-point star on Hamburg police caps. Home to eight thousand officers.

RAF

Red Army Faction. Left-wing extremist terrorist organization in Germany in 1970s and 1980s. Responsible for dozens of murders of politicians, businessmen, police officers, customs officials, and American soldiers, as well as kidnappings, hostage-takings, bank robberies, and bombings.

Rainbow

Multi-colored tablets that contain fentanyl (synthetic downer) and methamphetamine (synthetic upper) for sale to upper-class students. Ingestion can lead to heart attack or coma, particularly for non-addicts of heroin, cocaine, or speed.

Santa Fu

JVA Fühlsbüttel. Maximum security prison. After wartime tenure as concentration camp, went back to housing Hamburg's hardest criminals, like Sulejman Hasani. Coroner Rudi Deichmann is former coach of inmate soccer team.

SFP9-SF

Heckler & Koch Striker-Fired Pistol 9 – Special Forces. Short trigger reset favored by special ops, like GSG-9 veteran Thomas Ritter.

St. Pauli

    Red-light district at edge of Hamburg Harbor. Services foreign sailors and "respectable" citizens.

Steinwerder

    Island on Elbe River opposite St. Pauli. Built on rubble from Great Fire of 1842. Location of ship container refurbishing company. Where three bodies are found.

Theresienstadt

    Czech "settlement" established by SS in 1941 to mislead world about Final Solution. Wolf's grandparents were in camp's string quartet, while his mother took refuge in Hamburg.

U-Haft

    Untersuchungshaft. Pre-trial detention facility. Where three Hasani clan members are held after arrest by Thomas Ritter and Motz Beck.

PETER SARDA

Acknowledgements

Many thanks to the editors at Fiction Feedback for an extremely professional, insightful, and constructive critique. Special thanks to Dea Parkin of Fiction Feedback and the Crime Writers Association for very helpful advice and an incredibly thorough proofread. Finally, a big thank you to Phil Poole at 99designs for another killer cover.